'Look,' Annie said, 'I just want to see him – just to look at him, talk to him, find out what he's like.'

'Tell ya what he's like,' Billy said, wickedly glad for the opportunity. 'He's the one-in-a-million kid you dream about, that's what he's like. And you ain't about to see him – now or never!'

'Billy, just for an hour?'

She extended a hand and he shoved it away. 'No.'

He was dealing with a woman he knew well, and who knew him – or used to. He knew her not to be mean or spiteful, but neither was she dumb or weak. She could, in fact, be as tough as anybody he knew.

For some moments as they held each other's eyes, there was an electricity between them, an almost palpable current.

They both opened their mouths to speak at once, when T.J. came bursting out of the barn.

RICHARD WOODLEY

The Champ

A novel from
a screenplay by
Walter Newman
based on a story by
Frances Marion

FONTANA/Collins

First published in the United States in 1979 by
Dell Publishing Co Inc.
First published in Great Britain by Fontana Books 1979

Copyright © 1979 by Metro-Goldwyn-Mayer Inc.

Made and printed in Great Britain by
William Collins Sons & Co Ltd, Glasgow

CHAPTER 1

The old man with a flattened nose and one eye closed to a slit eased the plywood sheet off the front of the newsstand. In scrawled red paint across the plywood were the words: "KENNY'S NEWSSTAND." He slid it across the counter to the inside, letting it clatter to the floor.

"Gonna be hot," said another man coming up behind him.

"Yeah." No other traffic was on the sidewalk this early, and he had seen his friend from a long way off, trudging his way—just like most mornings. "Another hot one."

"Good day for the muscles, bad for the head."

"Oughta be out to the track." The old man stepped through the narrow doorway into the newsstand and arranged some boxes of gum and candy and some stacks of magazines on the counter. Then he leaned out, scanning the sky to the west of Miami where thunderheads were building over the Everglades. "That'll all pass to the north."

"You been out to the track yet?"

"Nope. Lotta action here. Lotta business. Lotta fighters."

"Bums." The second man, a bit younger than the first, jammed his hands into the pockets of his frayed topcoat and hunched his shoulders as if cold. His nose was bent to the left and he sniffed continually. "Know who I miss?" He yanked his left hand out of his pocket and hooked a fist through the air.

The old man inside the newsstand closed his good eye and nodded slowly. "Yeah."

"Know who I mean?"

"Yeah. Whassiz name."

"He was the best. Best I seen. Prince of the Ring they called him. What the hell . . ." The man looked at his fist, then opened his hand and scratched his head and looked off down the avenue. "You know?"

"Yeah. Ain't heard his name in a while."

"Ain't gonna, you old buzzard." The second man chuckled and hunched his shoulders under the top-coat. "Nothin' deader than a old title. Whole division's dead. Bet you couldn't name the top three light heavies."

"We got plenty comin' up. Lotta action inside the gym. You oughta go up and take a look some time."

"Bums. Why you open so early? Not even bums show up before eight."

"Gotta be ready. Gotta make a living." The old man looked at him through the slitted eye. "Ain't nobody gonna take care o' me but me, you know."

"Yeah." The second man looked away uncomfortably. "What you got on you?"

The old man felt around in his sweater pocket. "Smith Brothers black. What I chew for my cough." He held out the opened box.

"Thanks. What the hell's his name?" The man shook his head.

"Can't think of it myself."

They both looked off down the street and shook their heads.

"But he was the best."

"Yeah." The old man hoisted his arm and swung a weak left hook. "That's what he had." He smiled, closing his bad eye. "Know what he used to say? He said, 'I'll still be wearing the crown when they bulldoze this place.' He used to tell me that."

"Yeah. Well, they come, they go. We outlast 'em all. I gotta run."

"Come by later, I'll need a break."

"Yeah. Try'n think of his name."

"Yeah."

* * *

The hooves sliced through the rising mist in a blur and the noses puffed violent swirls of smoke as the horses, one after the other, leaned around the last turn and pounded into the stretch.

The men lining the rail sipped coffee, smoked, and leaned forward intently, their eyes squinting into the early sun. A few held stopwatches in front of them.

"Somebody time the chestnut with the bandages at the quarter pole?" one of them asked out of the corner of his mouth without turning his head.

"Check," said another down the line.

"I got the mare with the blinkers at the seven-eighth pole," said another, pulling the brim of his cap lower over his eyes.

The horses thundered by, exercise jockeys quickly rising over their saddles as they crossed the line. Eyes along the rail dipped to the watches.

"I got the bay filly in thirty-six and a few, Riley," said a clocker, shaking his head, "which is not so great."

"Not so great is right." Riley shoved his panama hat back on his head and rubbed away a line of sweat. "She looks beautiful, but beautiful don't mean she can run."

"Maybe the jock—"

"Naw. She shies in a crowd, don't like the pressure

in the turns. Nope. Be great for somebody's little girl."

"Maybe she can jump."

Riley scratched himself under his loose shirt. "Yeah." He turned around and leaned back against the white wooden railing and surveyed the empty grandstand. No breeze stirred the elegant royal palms and evergreens that rimmed the park; the pink flamingos and black swans were listless around the ponds of the infield. "Win some, lose some. The key to this game, my friend, is to know when to quit. Don't matter." He leaned over to brush some dust off his wrinkled slacks. "We're in pretty good shape down the line. I like the chestnut. Good workout." He ambled off toward the long barns of shed row.

The exercise jockeys, both now seated back on their tiny saddles, walked their mounts off the track. The rider of the chestnut angled over to pace beside the bay filly. "Hey, you pullin' up on that animal?"

"Pullin' up?" The rider squared his shoulders. "Me?"

"What I said."

"Hell no. I called on this booger for all she had but she was empty."

"I dunno. She sure looked pretty early on."

Other horses passed them heading for the track.

"All I know," said the rider on the filly, "is when I set her down, nothin' happened. Didn't wanna switch leads. She stayed on her left the whole damn way."

The other rider shrugged. They turned toward the barns, entering the area known as the backstretch.

The backstretch, behind the magnificent grandstand of the Hialeah racetrack, combined living quarters for boarded race horses as well as for people who worked with them. They lived a nomadic life, like circus people, following the racing season from track to track. The backstretch was a lively place, a place of common interests, where horse people mixed and chatted and shared deep understandings and loyalties beyond their work.

Horse heads stuck out of the open top halves of stable doors. Dogs and cats—stablemates for the highstrung thoroughbreds—wandered in and out of empty stalls, panting and purring gratefully for any passing attention they received. Chickens clucked and scratched the dirt and danced out of the way of horses and people. A blacksmith sorted out different sizes and styles of shoes on which he would work his hammer. Teen-age girls in dungarees and T-shirts walked blanketed horses back and forth in the moist dirt.

The two exercise riders nodded silently to the tall, strong blond man hotwalking a steaming horse, giving it time to cool down before being put back in its stall.

Billy Flynn nodded back mechanically, as mechanically as the horse behind him bobbed its head. But Billy's blue eyes didn't focus on them, or on anything. His attentions were focused on himself, inwardly. While it wouldn't have been apparent to the casual observer, Billy was engaged in a well-practiced and efficient routine.

He was taking stock of his physical self. In the rhythm of his walk, he took deep breaths, held them a few beats, let them out slowly. Under his clean white T-shirt he tensed and relaxed the round muscles of his shoulders and arms. He squeezed a rubber ball with his left hand for a few paces, then switched hands on the lead rope and squeezed the ball with his right. He rolled forward on his toes, sensing the litheness and bounce of his legs.

The messages he was receiving from his body were not altogether satisfactory; in other words, he was not in great shape. Certainly he was in *good* shape—tall and lean, with well-toned muscles, tapered from broad shoulders to narrow waist. At thirty-seven, he was in good shape, but not great. For he was not an ordinary thirty-seven-year-old man, but an ex-fighter; and he knew what being in great shape was, which was more than most ordinary men ever knew. His body was young, his face showed how old he was. It was not an old face, but the face of a fighter, which is not young.

He was by most standards handsome, or at least good-looking. His ears were not cauliflowered; his nose was straight, though thickened a bit on the sides. Some scar tissue limned the high edges of his cheekbones and rimmed his blue eyes. But he was not scarred much; he never cut easily. The overall effect was not to mar severely his good face but to give it the character that laugh lines or crow's feet sometimes do. His face was strong.

He blinked often. It was not vanity that kept him from wearing glasses, nor refusal to accept age. To wear glasses would allow his eyes to weaken further, he supposed. His vision was not blurred, but sometimes his eyes watered.

The messages he got from his body were that some parts were as strong as ever, some not, but that altogether great shape was within reach—which was what he wanted to know.

He began jogging the horse, running parallel to shed row.

"Attention," came the voice over the paddock public-address horn, "a reminder to all horsemen that nominations close Tuesday for the thirty-thousand-dollar Marina Handicap for three-year-olds upwards . . ."

Billy spat off to the side. Age was such a funny damn thing. In his business, it was lucky they didn't apply such firm age categories as they did with race horses.

His business. What the hell was his business? He spat again.

He slowed to a walk, then stopped, the horse halting fitfully behind him, dipping its head, then raising it high. Billy stiffened his legs and leaned over, reaching for the toes of his boots. He couldn't quite reach them and didn't care all that much. He liked how his lower back, upon which so much bobbing and weaving depended, could still snap him upright.

A radio rasped from back in one of the stalls. ". . . Hot and sunny, high expected of eighty-eight degrees. If you feel bad about Miami, just remember you could be in Buffalo. Okay, here's one from Edna and Roy out at Hialeah . . ."

Billy walked the horse in large circles.

". . . an update of an old song, third week on the charts, 'Stewball.' Okay, Edna, Roy, here's Garret Money's vocal . . ."

"Here, hon." Billy handed the lead rope to a girl who smiled at the horse and led it away. He walked around the corner of the barn, away from the radio, and leaned back against the warm brown planking. He squeezed the rubber ball hard, watching the cords rise over his arm. With his other hand he took a tin of aspirin out of his rear pocket, snapped it open, tossed a few uncounted tablets into his mouth, and chewed absently, staring across the active landscape of the backstretch.

A woman was sponging down the copper-toned hide of a filly. The woman, about his age, had a face older than that, lined and roughened like a drinker's, but alive and alert like a reformed one's. A husky woman with a long, fresh ponytail fixed with a pink bow behind her head, she was not unattractive. She hummed as she worked her sponge over the filly's flanks, and snatches of the tune reached Billy.

On the other side of the horse, he could see a small

11

boy's legs moving from side to side, which meant that he was helping. Billy reared back and heaved the ball high off toward the distant woods.

He walked over to the woman. "Josie, do me a little favor? Cover for me this afternoon? I got business in town."

"Sure, Billy." Her smile was bright and warm, deeply creasing her brown eyes. "Everything okay?"

"Okay?" He spat casually. "Hell, everything's great."

"Coming back tonight?"

"Yeah."

"Come up maybe?"

"Maybe."

She resumed sponging. "How you like She's A Lady?"

"Fine-looking filly."

"My favorite!" The boy popped from behind the horse, his blond hair sweaty, his freckles dancing in his smile.

"Hey, T.J." Billy mussed his hair.

"Hey, Champ."

"Well, Josie, thanks a lot. I'll—"

"Champ, you gonna do it?" T.J.'s face turned seriously expectant. "You gonna?"

Billy had started to turn away, now he stopped short and looked down at his son. He always watched impatiently for resemblances in T.J., and he was pleased. T.J. would be strong, unafraid. At eight, he was uncritically adoring of his father—guardian of the scrapbooks, shameless aper of his father's mannerisms. "What I'm thinkin', T.J., is I *listen* to the man. That's all."

T.J. waited for Billy to start walking away, then spat into the dirt and followed, stretching to keep up with Billy's long strides.

"Understand," Billy said back over his shoulder,

"all I say is *listen*. And if he makes good sense, which I doubt, *then* I consider."

"Charlie Goodman," T.J. said, enjoying the heft of the name on his lips, "he wants the Champ *bad!*"

"Take it easy, T.J." Billy stepped over a panting mutt, T.J. did the same. "I listen to the man, that don't mean I take the fight."

The mere mention of the fight caused T.J. to jab out a small right fist.

An exercise girl bent over to adjust the cinch of a tethered horse, jutting out a plump rear which Billy lightly swatted with the back of his hand. "You still hurtin', kid?"

"I broke up with him last night, Billy," she said, jumping a bit from the smack but not looking up. "You were right. No class."

Billy continued on. "Like I said, kid, not enough class for *you*."

A trio of tiny kittens nuzzled out from under the concrete walk beneath the portico of the barn. Billy stooped and took two of them gently by the skin on the back of their necks and hoisted them to peer into their pinched faces. "Coupla regular tigers."

T.J. picked up the third. "Yeah."

Billy stuffed the two back under the walk, heads first, shoving them close to their suckling mother. T.J. pushed his in with them.

"How come they always leave their momma?" T.J. asked.

"Not leave. They're just curious, can't leave the world alone."

"How come they ain't got no father?"

"They got a father, T.J." Billy chuckled. "He just don't hang around."

* * *

The calmness of Riley's telephone voice belied the

firmness with which he ran his horse-training business. He was a deliberate man, a fatalist who, as to people and horses, preferred the former as friends and the latter as business associates. Horses, he sometimes said, are dumb, but they don't argue back.

He closed his eyes and pushed his panama hat back on his head and sighed and leaned back in his creaky swivel chair and put his feet up on his cluttered desk. "I don't want to hear it, how the price of everything is up." He spoke evenly into the phone. "Yesterday it's the guy who does my shirts, today you tell me it's hay. I'd be better off feeding 'em my shirts."

His wife, Gloria, chuckled and nodded at him. She sipped coffee across the office—really a converted stall—near the small stove and refrigerator where hands came in for refreshment or to pass the time of day. Gloria's wide and pleasant face held no secrets, and Riley's shirts were a sight.

"So? It costs more to grow hay?" Riley abruptly dropped his feet to the floor and leaned over the desk. "You some kind of star in the hay business? I got nothin' to think about. You think about it. You come up with a price, call me later."

He banged the phone down more rudely than usual, then brightened quickly upon seeing Billy and T.J. standing at the door. "Billy, the plain sight of you makes me feel better!" He grinned through a day's growth, wrinkling up his tanned face. He motioned them in avidly. "How come nothing bothers you, huh? What's the secret?"

"Well, I tell ya, Mr. Riley"—Billy shrugged as he stepped in, T.J. right behind him—"no matter how bad things are, no matter what trouble I'm in, I can always make myself feel good remembering one thing."

Riley raised his gray eyebrows and leaned back.

"Today I don't hafta go to school."

"Haw!" Riley shook his head and rasped a finger over his chin. Gloria chuckled and waved T.J. over and put an arm around his waist. T.J. was the only person in the backstretch who would ordinarily be in school, and Josie had taught him how to read and write and add and subtract.

Riley slid out of his chair and around the desk and cuffed Billy's left shoulder with a light punch.

Billy dipped almost imperceptibly to the side. "You step inside with that right, I'm gonna nail you. I told you that a hundred times." He feinted a left hook, and they all laughed.

Riley slapped him on the back and returned to his chair, flopping down on it noisily. "Wouldn't take much, Billy, to spread an old man like me over the ropes. What's on your mind?"

"Uh, well, Mr. Riley"—Billy scratched his chest— "I'd like the afternoon off. Josie said she'd cover for me."

"Important, is it?" Riley's smile disappeared. "Business?"

"Business."

Riley narrowed his eyes, picked up a pencil and fingered it with both hands. "You really gonna do it this time?"

"Maybe. Maybe not." Billy glanced over at T.J., whose eyes were fixed on him as he knew they would be. "Nothing definite. For the right terms it's a possibility."

"Possibility." Riley pushed out his lips and studied the pencil. "You got a lot of friends here who would hate to see if you go on the one hand and love to see you go on the other, if you know what I mean. Lot of your friends here would love to see you back on top."

"Nobody should get their hopes up, either way."

Riley chuckled, then smiled up at him. "Sure, Billy,

take the afternoon. Just let me be the first to know."

"Billy," Gloria called over, "you're not going to let T.J. eat this garbage, are you?"

T.J., without missing a word of the conversation, had opened the pastry box and lifted out a glazed donut, which was now poised near his mouth. He looked at Billy.

"Ordinarily no," Billy said, turning to leave, "but I can see from here those are health donuts."

T.J. immediately chomped down on a big bite of the donut, leaving shiny flakes of sugar on his chin. He strode quickly after Billy.

At the door, Billy stopped and turned back, unsmiling. "Thanks, Mr. Riley. Appreciate."

Riley waved him off. "No problem. Wait." He rose quickly and went over, taking Billy by the shoulder and walking him outside. "Look," he said confidentially, "you feel like going back in the ring, maybe you should. Who am I to say? I don't know what you got or what you need, if you know what I mean. But just be careful, Billy—give it some thought."

"I'm thinking."

"You're thirty-seven." Billy stiffened. "Last time you fought you were thirty." Riley lowered his head quickly. "I don't mean—"

"Truth. I know. But I still got the moves. Hell"—Billy stepped back and spread his arms—"Doc calls me a medical marvel."

"Well, Doc's a vet." Riley studied him.

"He knows, though. Wolcott was thirty-seven when he took the heavyweight title. Ali was—"

"I know, Billy, I know."

"Archie Moore, he fought until he was what? Fifty?" Billy daubed at his watering eyes with the back of his hand.

"I know that too. Of course. All I'm saying is none of those guys laid off seven years."

"I ain't exactly been layin' *down*." Billy tensed his arms and rotated his shoulders, smiling thinly.

Riley watched him, brightened, grabbed his right shoulder and squeezed. "Twelve hundred bucks I win off you in the Frank Cox fight."

"Stone cold left hook in the eighth." Billy snapped a short, taut left hook through the air.

"You were beautiful, Billy." Riley turned away, looked down at T.J., and flicked some sugar off the boy's cheek with an index finger. "I remember watching your fights and saying to myself, 'My God, this Flynn, he's blessed with such talent.' I figure you hold the title five more years at least—nobody on the horizon can touch you. But one bad fight, you lose it, you walk away. . . ." His voice trailed off. He looked away and scratched his neck.

Billy sniffed, glanced at T.J.

"Imagine the dough I didn't make," Riley mused softly, "in the years you been off." His tone was not accusatory. Riley, in fact, was sorry he brought it up.

"Look, I gotta go, Mr. Riley."

Riley plunged a hand into his trouser pocket and pulled out a lump of bills and stripped a twenty from it. "Take this." He crumpled it and tried to shove it into Billy's hand.

"Aw, no." Billy stepped back and held up his hands. "Honest."

"Come on—for gloves, expenses, it's nothing!" He paused, then nodded, seeing that Billy was firm on it, and knowing well his pride. "Okay, okay—but don't ever be afraid to ask."

"I ain't afraid."

"No." Riley slapped Billy's neck gently. "Good luck, Billy."

"Thanks."

T.J. mouthed the same word silently.

* * *

The morning hours passed with agonizing slowness for T.J. He raced from chore to chore, anything to keep busy. He helped his old black friend Beau muck out a stall, helped Josie sponge down some horses, cleaned tack, fed the dogs.

T.J. had never seen a boxing match, except on TV. So he knew nothing about the sounds and smells of the fighters, the pains and cuts, the sweat and the breathing, the feral surge of the crowd at ringside, except for how it all seemed on twelve inches of black and white. But from watching with his father, he knew a lot about strategy, nuances of the course of a fight. More than those in the crowd at a fight, he knew what was happening. He knew what punches were being slipped or landing ineffectively, even when the crowd at ringside did not. He knew who was not pacing himself right; who was dropping his hands; who was the aggressor; who was better able to take and deliver a body punch; who had turned the fight around since the fifth when he asserted a stinging left jab; who was better inside or on the ropes; who needed the knockout in the tenth to win.

But none of this was associated with punishment. That meant that T.J., while understanding the strategy, could not really understand why some fighters didn't correct obvious flaws during a fight. He could not sense, as did his father, the agonizing exhaustion, the fatal weariness that more than anything else dictated how much a fighter was able to alter, adapt, come on in the crucial late rounds. Easy enough to see why blood dribbling into an eye could obscure a fighter's vision and make it tough. Harder to grasp the struggle to breathe when less visible blood inside the mouth or nose clogged you up. Fighters knew, Billy knew; T.J. knew to the extent that he knew it was not good to get cut. And a good corner man could save a fighter from effects of a cut.

So to T.J. fighting was simply not that complicated. Not when you had a father like Billy who knew it all, who had been champion of the world, who had arms like iron and an iron will to match. Not when you had a father who everybody said could lick all these pretenders in his prime. And there was nothing T.J. could see to suggest that the Champ was in anything less than his prime. Whether thirty or thirty-seven, those numbers meant nothing to a boy of eight.

Finally the big Seth Thomas clock on the stable wall showed it was time. T.J. slammed his curry comb and brush down into the box and dashed out of the barn and down the path, scattering chickens. He pounded up the rickety wooden staircase, burst through the screen door, and stood for a few seconds panting in their second-floor living quarters.

It was just a room. Windows on two sides, naked plasterboard nailed onto wooden walls. Two single beds aligned near each other. TV on a crate. Bathroom and shower concealed by a plywood partition. Calendar on the wall. Sink, small gas stove, half-size refrigerator. A few fight photographs pinned up. The one of which they both were proudest was of Billy, head and shoulders glistening with sweat, greasy skin-colored patch above his right eye, blond hair matted under the hand of some unseen attendant, staring straight into the camera with just a hint of a smile from puffy lips just after winning the championship.

T.J. removed the TV and snatched the wooden crate under it and slid it across the floor to the closet—a cubicle in the corner covered by a curtain. He hopped up on the crate, pushed the curtain aside, and felt above him along the high shelf. He searched quickly with his hand.

He stopped, thought for a moment, then leaped

down and scurried across to the bed on his hands and knees. Rear high in the air, he pushed his head under the bed. The he backed out, bumping his head on the bed frame but not noticing that. For he had found it, a dusty cardboard box.

He hugged the box to his chest and laughed silently. Then he tucked the box under one arm and ran out, the clap of his footfalls on the stairs ending even before the screen door had time to slam shut above him.

* * *

Billy closed his eyes languorously and rubbed his forehead with a thumb and forefinger, pinching the skin above his brows. A tic over the eyes annoyed him. He leaned back roughly against his tomato-red 1968 Cadillac convertible with its ragged top down. He shifted his body uneasily within the unaccustomed outfit he termed "classy garbage."

He was wearing a beige-check leisure suit, well tailored and creased, over a salmon-pink shirt, on the left breast of which was monogrammed in red, "BF." His alligator loafers glistened. He looked splendid, as if the outfit were made for him, as indeed it had been, and was the last remaining segment of the wardrobe assembled during his glory years. He squirmed slightly with embarrassment in the knowledge that those most familiar with him would recognize the outfit as being his only one for dress. His pride those earlier years had been to don different outfits or different mixes for each occasion.

He absently checked the crease in his trousers, crossed his legs and arms, and looked up to see T.J. trotting across the yard toward him, blond hair bouncing, arm cradling a package.

"I been looking all over for ya," T.J. called breathlessly.

"It's *you*, not *ya*," Billy corrected. "How many times I haveta say that? And hustle it up or I'll be late."

T.J. reached his side, panting, and looked up at him.

"What's in the box?"

T.J. smiled brightly and held it up. "Something from the silks shop. They made it up *special*."

Billy took the box suspiciously, narrowing his eyes. "What's so special it has to be made up in the silks shop?"

"Well, *look*!" T.J. danced from one foot to the other. "Go ahead, open it!"

Billy pulled off the string, still eyeing T.J., then lifted the top. He blinked slowly. Carefully he took out a black silk robe, dropped the box, and held the robe out at arm's length. Large white letters across the back spelled BILLY FLYNN—THE CHAMP.

Billy held it stiffly, his mouth open. He stared at the inscription, his eyes playing over it from left to right, right to left, taking in the testimony to past status.

"Like it?" T.J.'s eyes were wide and expectant. "Like it?"

"Sure I like it," Billy said softly, now stroking the robe with one hand, feeling the delicate sheen, so paradoxical for a sweating boxer's broad back. Silk robes always seemed to belie the violent bodies they covered; but in this business they were worn like ensigns—colors, cut, and letters announcing the style and confidence of the wearer. You had to have a fine robe, and this was one. "I like it very much. Wow!" He patted T.J.'s cheek. "But how much—"

"Come on, you ain't supposed to ask that. I saved. You really like it?" T.J. danced.

"You know I do." He slapped the side of T.J.'s head affectionately. "It's beautiful." Then he tossed the robe over T.J.'s shoulder and turned to the car. "Come on, pack it up for me and let's haul." He slid behind the wheel while T.J. quickly stuffed the robe back into the box and tossed it into the back seat.

T.J. trotted around and slid in beside him. "Gonna make a comeback!" he yelled happily over the first roar of the big engine.

"Comeback? Comeback hell!" Billy slapped the wheel, grinning. "Comeback's for has-beens. And I'm no has-been, right?"

"Right!" T.J. slapped the dash gleefully. "Right on, Champ!"

They wound through the familiar Miami streets, Billy commenting gruffly as usual on the growing Latin influence on the city. He was not hostile to Cubans or Haitians or Panamanians, was neither political nor bigoted. It was the change that unsettled him. Change made him feel older. He could remember when this section was different, when there were regular diners and restaurants instead of "La" this and "La" that and shops filled with religious figurines.

Even the size of the people disturbed him. Latin fighters, tough as they often were, seemed usually bred for the smaller divisions. And to Billy, anything under light heavy was not serious. How could he take fighters seriously when, good as they were in their lesser divisions, they could not dare to climb into the ring with somebody his size?

And at six feet two, one hundred and eighty—which made him a heavyweight now—he was tall but not all that huge. He knew there were Latin fighters bigger than he, and good. And a few not as big were super. Duran, for example, from Panama. Maybe the best, pound for pound, in the world. A lightweight, but a tiger and a treat to watch. He welcomed good fighters, enjoyed seeing them from wherever. But he hated to see Miami change, or anything around him for that matter. He sometimes wished time would stop for a while, just till he got back in high gear.

They left the car in a lot and walked up the street to the Fifth Street Gym, a well-used, fading, and pleasantly familiar old building where some of the best fighters of the century had trained.

They stopped in front of the small, dilapidated wooden newsstand just outside the downstairs entrance to the gym.

"Hey, Kenny, whaddaya say?" Billy smiled in at the old man with the slitted eye and flattened nose.

"Billy!" His one eye widened with the sudden recall of the name he hadn't been able to remember that morning. "Hi, Billy!"

"Keepin' your left up?"

"Yeah, yeah." Kenny raised a left fist protectively alongside his jaw. He leaned out from among the magazines and candy bars. When he smiled, ancient scar tissue around his eyes and mouth wriggled. His tongue was thick, speech slow, the result of more than two hundred fights long years ago. He sniffed through his flattened nose. "I remember, yeah."

"Hi, Billy!" A small black face appeared above the counter, the face of Sonny, a boy of twelve, Kenny's almost constant companion, who came around every day to help Kenny with the business—count change and read labels too faint for Kenny's dim eyes.

"Hi, Sonny. So how goes it, Kenny?"

Kenny rocked unevenly from side to side on his toes. "Always onna level. Yours truly, Kenny Hansen. Ain't seen you around here in a while, Billy."

"You know how it is, Kenny. Business. Always business."

"Yeah." Kenny continued rocking and awkwardly rotating his shoulders as if loosening up. "Same way with me. Busy." He kept his eyes fixed on Billy.

"Uh, you got the new *Ring* in there, Kenny?"

"Yeah, sure," he said quickly. "Just come in yesterday. Right in here." He turned away and rummaged through a pile of dusty, faded magazines, extracting one from near the top. "Right here." Holding it in both hands, he placed it reverently on the counter in front of Billy. "Last one, guess you're in luck."

It was the right month, but a couple of years old, a fact that neither surprised nor bothered Billy. He was never sure whether old Kenny was faking, hustling, or just couldn't see the dates on the magazines, but it didn't matter. He was a beat-up old coot, had paid his dues many times over, and like so many fighters had nothing to show for it except scars and damaged wits. And like so many others in the business over the decades, he had not been much of a fighter, but more of a fighter than anything else. Rough as it was fighting your way to the top, it was far rougher fighting always near the bottom. Worse fighters took worse beatings. The irony to Billy was, the worse you were, the more dues you paid, and the less you ended up with.

"Glad to see my luck is still holding, Kenny." Billy handed him a five dollar bill, which Kenny took without comment.

"That's a five," Sonny piped up softly. "*Ring's* only one."

"Oh." Kenny looked down at the bill, then up at Billy. "Sorry, we can't break a five just now."

"Who asked for change?" It was a game they played. "Come on, just take it and relax."

"Aw, no, Billy—"

"Don't give me a hard time now"—Billy cocked a left—"or I give you one right here." His fist gently clipped Kenny's big jaw.

Kenny bobbed away, stumbling, and giggled. "You're something, Billy, a regular sweetheart."

"Sweetheart, huh?" Billy gave him an arch frown. "That a fact? And who the hell are you? A petunia?"

Kenny stood up straight, squaring his shoulders. "Always onna level," he said with some dignity. "Yours very truly, Kenny Hansen."

They turned away toward the entrance, Billy shaking his head and T.J. doing likewise. Once inside the door, Billy tossed the old *Ring* into a trashcan, and they headed up the steps.

Billy took the stairs slowly, savoring the first sounds of slaps and thuds, the first smells of liniment from above. On the top landing was a small table, onto which was bolted a cashbox with a few coins in it. A sign propped up next to it said ADMISSION 50¢. Billy ignored the box but stopped to shake hands with the gaunt man behind it.

"Billy Flynn, well damn me!"

"Hey, Jinx. Good ta see ya."

Then he and T.J. stepped through the door. It was all there, just as he remembered it. Billy leaned back against the wall and smiled faintly.

Dominating the big room were two elevated rings where fighters were sparring, wearing headguards and wide protective belts and big fourteen-ounce training gloves. Their trunks were stained with sweat and dirt. Around the floor of the gym other fighters jumped rope with rhythmic pit-a-pats; some punched the small speed bags suspended above their heads, others thumped their fists into the big bags or into padded mitts held by handlers. Sweat and liniment glistened on their bodies, and the smell pervaded the room and bathed Billy in its familiar promise of action and hope. He felt at home.

He ambled into the room, glancing at the posters and pictures on the wall, showing fighters from long ago. A few fighters stopped what they were doing to look at him. He was still known to many.

"How's it goin', Champ!"

"Lookin' good, Champ, still lookin' good . . ."

"Long time no see, Champ."

Billy nodded casually, his practiced eye sizing up builds, speeds, conditions of the fighters around the room. Then he turned his attention to the rings.

In one ring it was a white fighter against a Latin. In the other it was a Latin against a black. They grunted and stomped around, slapping and pounding each other wearily, while onlookers leaned against the ring aprons and nodded or shook their heads or called advice and encouragement. Punches thudded off the headguards covering the cheeks, off the big leather belts protecting the kidneys, off the bare midsections.

Timers at ringside clanged their hammers against steel automobile wheel rims, making a loud "gong" that ended the rounds. The fighters went to their corners to lean against the ropes, sweat dripping onto the canvas mats from their drooping heads and heaving chests.

One of the timers, a short, stocky, pug-nosed man wearing an applejack cap, caught sight of Billy, did a double take, then hurried over. "Billy! How goes it! I don't believe I'm seein' ya here!"

"Hey, Hesh," Billy said, the two of them seizing each other's arms in strong grips.

"You look good, Billy, real good." Hesh leaned back to look at him. "And who's this here?" He bent over in front of T.J. "Don't tell me this is T.J.!"

"Yup, that's T.J.," Billy said with quiet pride.

"I don't believe it! You know who I am, T.J.?"

"Yup. You're Hesh. The Champ told me about you."

"What did he tell you, come on."

"He said you were a good man to have in your corner."

"Hey!" Hesh pinched T.J.'s shoulder. "How 'bout that? Come on, T.J.!" Hesh held his arms away and thrust his midsection forward. "Gimme a good one, right here in the old solar plexus!"

Glancing first at his father, T.J. reached back and drove his fist into Hesh's belly.

"Ow! Oooh!" Hesh stumbled backwards, hands on his belly. "Again!"

T.J. dug another right into Hesh's fleshy midsection.

"Enough! I quit!" Hesh waved his arms. T.J. grinned. Then Hesh moved up to Billy, taking his arm. "Billy, you mean it this time? Huh?" he asked softly. "You comin' back?"

"Maybe." Billy edged away and stepped up closer to the nearest ring, leaning on his elbows over the apron as the next round began.

The Latin came out fast and smashed a hard left to the ribs of the white fighter, following with a quick right to the side. The white fighter winced, backed off a step, tried to counter with two jabs to keep the Latin away. The Latin ducked, feinted with the right, then struck a stiff left straight to the mouth.

The white fighter blinked. His pink mouthpiece showed a darker tinge of red. He kept backing up, jabbing, covering up, jabbing some more. The Latin bored in, ignoring the jabs, pounding both hands to the body, raising welts on the white skin.

Billy watched intensely, twitching slightly with empathy for those body blows. "Right uppercut," he muttered toward the white fighter, "you gotta straighten him up."

The onlookers near Billy nodded deferentially.

Billy closed his eyes for a second, then moved over to the second ring.

Here too the Latin was boring in. Billy recognized the typical style they had—nothing fancy, but keep coming at you. But the black fighter was a good dancer. No Ali, to be sure, but quick and light, with a sure, snappy jab. His left kept popping off the Latin's headguard and face—whap, whap, whap. Blood streamed from the Latin's nostrils as his head snapped back again and again from the jabs he took while trying to come in. Eventually, Billy thought, the Latin would break through the black fighter's cute style.

Again Billy closed his eyes. He hadn't felt the pain for a while, and was abruptly reminded that it started here in the gym and never ended, the pain of getting hit. With each smack of leather to leather, leather to flesh, he felt his gut tighten. His hands clenched. His eyes watered. The skin over his cheekbones danced with nerves.

T.J., at first excited and awed by all the action and noise, glanced up at his father in wonder, then in concern at the pained expression, the closed eyes. He dared not speak. This was his father's place, a world he didn't really understand. Whatever his father felt here, watching the fighters, was something T.J. had no right to ask about.

A spare, stooped man of about seventy with thin, slicked-back white hair appeared at Billy's side wheeling a supermarket shopping cart filled with boxing equipment. "Got everything for ya right here, Billy," he said, his voice nervous. "And I got a locker and everything for ya. Go right in and change." As he spoke, the man jabbed a gnarled finger in the air, punctuating his words.

Billy looked at the cart. There were high-topped shoes, training gloves, a small "peanut" punching bag, a water bottle, a headguard, protective belt, various handwraps, and tubes of ointment. He stared dumbly at the assortment for a moment, then blinked and wakened to what he was seeing. "What's all this, Georgie? Goodman show yet?"

"He ain't showed. Here, Billy." He jabbed his finger at the cart. "Got yer trunks, shoes, everything. I'll be in the corner for ya, and—"

"What's this garbage, I gotta work out?" Billy slapped the cart away. "I gotta show him what I got?

Didn't he make enough money off me, all the times I fought?"

Georgie blinked at him and moved his lips nervously.

"A champ, he wants to see *me* work?" Billy's look grew fierce, and Georgie backed off a step, wiggling his nose like a rabbit. "It's pure crap and I won't do it!" He kicked at the cart. "And I'm not gonna be sittin' around waitin' for him neither!" Billy spun away to face the ring and put his fists on the apron. "What I gotta say? 'Gee, Charlie, so good to see you, Charlie, thanks for the big fat break you're givin' me outta the goodness of your heart'!"

Georgie glanced around, then dared forward a step and tapped his finger on Billy's arm. "So what I tell him, Champ?"

"Tell him what I just said and that I went out for a walk. He can wait for *me*!" He started toward the door. "Be back in a half hour."

T.J., trying to hide his concern and confusion, started after him.

Billy held up a palm. "You stay here." Then he tried to smile. "What's the matter? You figure four o'clock in the afternoon on Fifth Street I'm gonna get mugged?" He reached out and tousled T.J.'s hair, then moved to the door, where he stopped again and looked back at the ring.

It was the far ring that drew his attention. The drama he had expected was being played out. Trouble with so many young fighters was that all they thought they had to do was copy some champ's moves. They thought it was simple. They didn't know what went into it, what was behind it. If you wanted to stick and move, you had to stick hard and move quick. Dancers like Sugar Ray or Ali didn't just dance, they stuck and slipped, bobbed and weaved and stuck again, hard. And the punch was always right there,

29

minute you dropped your guard. They were artists at slipping your shots, frustrating you, wearing you down while they beat you up. Kind of fighters that destroyed your will by seeming able to fight you forever. And the bottom line was that they could always put you away with one or two good shots.

That was the difference between champs and chumps. Not many champs in this world, but a whole lot of chumps. That was why so many of these Latins, with their straight-ahead style, won fights. And that was what Billy was seeing now. The Latin had at last worked the juking, dancing black into a corner and was doubling him up with two-handed punishment to the body. A real fight would be about over here. Whether or not the black dancer was knocked out, he was finished. Body shots that hurt like that you never recovered from—not in ten rounds, not in fifteen. The black was hurting. Billy winced and closed his eyes. He tensed his own body muscles, wondering if they could still withstand the siege of fists.

Yes, they could. But they wouldn't have to. Billy would never let himself get backed up like that. He was too slick. He could move *and* punch. Good left jab, good quick uppercut to straighten up a fighter like that, and move in. Billy always moved. He was not a punching bag—always that good lateral movement, head never a still target—but a puncher. He always established that from the opening bell. Move and dance, but let them know right away he could hurt them. Right away. Take their best shot early, see if they could take his. He could, they couldn't. Not seven years ago. Not now.

He slid quickly through the door and trotted down the stairs.

"Hey, Billy, how's it goin' today, Billy?"

Billy walked past Kenny, not seeing or hearing him, head down, hands jammed in pockets. Then, several yards beyond, he stopped, took a deep breath, and took out the tin, from which he shook several aspirin into his mouth.

T.J. remained in the gym as instructed. But he slunk away from the sparring rings, back to the wall, and sat down on a bench. He tried to watch the fighters in the rings, but couldn't. The violence became ugly to him, without the Champ there. He watched the men work out with bags and jump ropes and wondered if that really had anything to do with fighting, and whether you could tell a good fighter from a bad one in that exercise, and whether the Champ would have to go through all that before a fight.

He tried to imagine his father jumping rope and hitting the speed bag. Somehow it didn't seem right for the Champ to have to do that. He would just climb into the ring and knock somebody out. T.J. couldn't imagine the Champ getting hit. He could only see him knocking somebody out. He wished the Champ were there with him, beside him, because the place sure was loud and lonely and scary without him.

CHAPTER 2

Billy walked slowly down the street, past run-down shops, a boarded-up movie house, a beanery with greased windows. Music came from a record store. "'Stewball,'" he muttered, remembering the record that had intruded upon his reverie while he'd walked the horse that morning. "Greaseball. Mouthball. Spitball!" He spat off to the side. A passing shower had left the sidewalks wet, and thunderheads now moved off to the northeast.

A small, thin man sidled up to him, glancing quickly right and left before speaking. "Looking for something, mister?"

"Beat it."

The man shoved a small card at him. "Got something for you, mister. She can do it all."

"I said—" Billy's left fist was cocked before he realized it, and he instantly brought his hand down. But the man had already fled, darting up an alley. "Jesus." Billy shook his head. Nerves. Should never let that happen. Fists are weapons in this business. Little punk almost caused trouble for them both. Never happened before. Ordinarily he was calm and under control. What the hell was bugging him so much?

He stopped and looked around. He had wandered a ways. He had forgotten his watch, but that was okay. Time wasn't with him anyway.

Charlie Goodman had no right. Who the hell was he? Crummy, two-bit promoter after a quick buck. Make the Champ work out, make him wait. Billy had nothing against promoters wanting to cash in— why not? Business was business. But don't waste the Champ's time, because business was business for him too. And he would be the one to climb through those ropes. He would be the one to do the hard work, take and deliver the punches, pay everybody's bills. In the end, everything rested on the Champ's shoulders. And Charlie had no right to make him wait and set his nerves on edge like this. Promoters should promote; he would do the fighting. Right now he wanted to take the edge off.

The flickering neon in the dingy window said DRAFT. Billy walked in and slid onto a stool. "Seven and a glass, Luis," he said.

The bartender mechanically reached for the Seagram's bottle, poured a shot, then drew a draft beer from the imitation wood cask, and shoved them both across the counter.

If Jackie were here, his old trainer Jackie from Chicago, he would make everything go smooth, and Billy wouldn't have to worry about anything except the fight. Billy could relax and do his job. But Jackie was not here. This was the other way to relax. Billy threw down the shot.

* * *

T.J. had been watching the door, hoping to see Billy return. The old cornerman Georgie stepped into his line of vision and beckoned. T.J. hopped up from the bench. "What?"

"Office," Georgie said, again hooking his finger at him and starting away across the floor.

T.J. followed quickly. They went through a loose-hung door and Georgie closed it behind them. A short,

round man with a scraggly dark mustache and hair
parted in the middle sat on the desk chewing an unlit
cigar. He nodded to them, crossing his stubby legs.

"You're T.J.," the man said, nodding. "I'm Charlie
Goodman. Where the hell's your old man?"

T.J. shrugged. It always took him a few moments
to summon his manliness. The idea was, he had
learned from the Champ, when on somebody else's
turf to say as little as possible while holding your
ground. Don't get into anything until you know what
you're getting into. His job here was to cover for the
Champ. Goodman didn't awe him; the Champ never
thought much of guys who would wear white socks
with a suit.

Goodman checked his watch, put his palms down
on the desk and rocked back and forth. "Okay, so
Billy don't want to go a few rounds for me. I can
see that. I don't have to be beat over the head." He
tapped his head with a pudgy finger and shifted the
cigar from one corner of his mouth to the other,
dislodging a bead of saliva that came to rest halfway
down his chin. "Billy was a great fighter, and a great
fighter has his pride. But now he's a half hour late
and it's beginning to get to me."

He eyed T.J. as if he had delivered a question.

"He said something about shirts," T.J. said quickly,
shifting his feet and glancing at Goodman. "Maybe he
went to pick up the laundry." It was lame, but T.J. was
briefly proud of it.

Goodman, though, didn't react at all to the ploy.
"I'm a gentleman, he's a gentleman," he said, waggling
his cigar in his mouth, "so we wait." He smiled a little
meanly at T.J. Goodman was not a mean man, however
mean his business, but it's hard to smile warmly
around a damp cigar. In fact, he rather admired the
pluck of the little fellow. He studied T.J. as he now
lit his cigar, waving the match slowly back and forth

under the tip. He liked Billy too, in the way you dared like fighters, which was in a business way, nothing personal. Billy was tough and straight, which he liked; thirty-seven, which he didn't. Maybe he had a good fight or two left in him, maybe not. Well promoted, though, the ex-champ could pack a house. Goodman liked the kid, liked the way he stood up for the old man. But he wished there weren't a kid involved. Kids were worse than wives in this business. They got in the way. He relit his cigar and widened his lips in a grin, showing teeth. "Maybe he's arguin' about too much starch in his shirts."

T.J. shrugged. His mouth felt dry.

* * *

Billy took a swallow of beer, followed it quickly with the shot, then drained the beer and slid both glasses toward the bartender. "'Nother, Luis."

The Cuban woman perched on the stool next to him hitched her purse back over her shoulder with one hand and ran her fingers down Billy's broad back with the other. Billy pulled his shoulders forward and arched his back, like a cat being petted.

He tossed down the next shot and sipped from the beer glass. "Stories? You want stories?" The bartender, also Cuban, leaned across the bar and nodded with a smile. "Oh, the worthless SOB had stories!" He cocked his head at the woman and smiled obliquely. "Curl your hair—not that either of you need more curl than you got!" He guffawed wetly.

The woman touched her teased mop and licked her heavily glossed lips. She glanced privately at her watch, then at the door, then leaned back toward Billy.

He noticed everything. "Plenty of time, plenty. Early yet. You'll have business all night. Hit me again, Luis!" He slid his shot glass over the bar. "One for Carmen

Miranda here too!" He looked at her. "What're the prices around here now anyway? Whatcha gettin'?"

She hardened her eyes a bit. Billy cleared his throat. "Never mind. Shouldn'ta asked. None a my business. Thanks, Luis."

The woman nodded her thanks also and pulled the shot daintily in front of her.

"Now then, about my old friend." Billy put an arm around the woman and pulled her over, causing her almost to lose her balance on the stool. "He loved Havana. Loved it. Six months at sea, and pay he had comin'. My friend would grab that and head right for Havana. What a place, in those days, he told me."

"I remember," Luis said, shaking his head and winking at the woman. "Never be the same. Right, Rosey?"

The woman smiled briefly and shyly, looking at her glass while trying to hitch back onto her stool.

Billy held her tight with one arm. "One girl he told me about, she had this little toy poodle." He pulled her head down and caused them both to lean across toward Luis conspiratorially. He lowered his voice. "Had the fur dyed pink. Pink! Can you imagine that? Like a lollipop! Trained it too. Damn thing would sit on the edge of the bed and watch, make these little sounds, whines, you know? Like he wanted some of the action!"

He slapped the bar, causing Luis and the woman to flinch. Then he released her, leaned back, and laughed.

Luis laughed too. He hooked a thumb at the woman. "Sounds like her mother."

They all laughed, Billy pounding his palm on the bar.

The woman put her arms around Billy's neck and

planted a kiss on his cheek and ran her fingers through his hair.

"Easy now," Billy said, pushing her hand away. "Kisses okay, but don't mess with the hair." Then he pulled her back. "Everybody wants a piece of the Champ. 'Specially all you south-of-the-border chumps with no country of your own."

Abruptly Billy sat up straight, palms planted on the bar. He looked straight at Luis. "This country's great," he said sternly.

"Yes it is," Luis said, quickly bringing forth a rag with which he mopped the area between them.

"Gives everybody a chance to make somethin' outta it."

"That's right." Luis refilled the glasses.

"Champs and chumps, everybody got a chance to make it back. Hit us again, Luis!"

"You already got it." Luis pointed to the glasses.

Billy sat musing while the woman idly turned her shot glass in her fingers. "Know what, Luis? Gonna bring everybody right back in here, right back in your little place here, afterwards. To celebrate, you know? We go back a long time, but I never did that before. You prolly never had *nobody* do that before."

"Nope." Luis shook his head.

"Yup. Be right back in here after I make it. It's friendly. That's what makes this country great. Free for everbody."

"Right." Luis rubbed his chin.

"Make what, Billy?" It was the first thing the woman had said in a long time.

"Shuddup, broad." Billy grinned at her. "And gimme another kiss, one a them Latino numbers, dyed pink." She pecked him on the cheek, then sat back up straight. He pulled up his shirt sleeve. "Forgot my watch." He waved his arm grandly. "Don't matter.

Plenty a time." He looked at her seriously. "Training's the roughest."

She nodded and looked questioningly at Luis.

"When's the band come in?" Billy fluttered a hand toward the bandstand at the end of the bar.

"While."

"'Cause I got a headache from sittin' around too long. You know why?" He made a fist with his right hand and held it in front of the woman. "Made for action."

He winced and took out his tin and dumped some aspirin on the bar, scooped them up, and chewed them. The woman snapped open her purse, took out a cigarette, and leaned forward for Luis to light it.

"I don't smoke neither," Billy said. "You know why?" The woman swallowed her smoke and raised her eyebrows. He leaned toward her. "'Cause I'm never more'n *that far* . . ."—he held up his two index fingers like goalposts—"from bein' in top shape. Thass why."

"You look good." She lowered her eyelids.

"Haw." Billy snorted. "You don't know. How I look is all in *here*"—he tapped his skull—"and *here*"—he tapped his chest. "Head and heart, thass where a fighter *lives!*"

"You're a fighter, then?"

"Holy Jesus, Luis! Don't she know what we been talkin' about all this time?"

"You ain't said nothing to her, Billy."

Billy pushed out his lips and tightened his arms so that the muscles rippled. "Thass because I let my *fiss* do the talkin'!"

* * *

Goodman mashed out his cigar stub. "Well, maybe he got hit by a car. A bus even. Sorry, kid, didn't mean it really."

T.J. stood quietly, staring at the floor.

"Well, kid, I tell you, it's a great pity." Goodman sighed and stood up, pulled the cuffs down on his shirt sleeves, dusted the cigar ash off his front, and went over to the coat rack to take his suit jacket. "A great pity indeed. This was gonna be a genuine dream fight. Small fortune for us all. Billy Flynn in the comeback of the century, and as a heavyweight to boot. But no Billy." He pulled on his jacket, sighing again.

Georgie wrung his hands and paced nervously. "This just ain't like the Champ. T.J. says he gets up every morning at four thirty on the dot. Like he has a clock in his head."

"Always four thirty," T.J. chimed in anxiously. "Not a minute later."

"Maybe something's screwed up with his clock then. He took a lot of shots that last fight."

"No!" T.J.'s eyes were wet. "He's in good shape!"

Georgie stepped up to Goodman and put a shaky hand on his sleeve. "Maybe, Charlie, ten minutes more. One minute for each of the ten times he fought for you, huh?"

"Fifteen minutes, Mr. Goodman," T.J. pleaded. "It's so important. Something funny musta happened."

"Well—"

"Just fifteen minutes!" T.J. hopped in front of him. "Please gimme fifteen minutes. I'll find him!"

Goodman took a deep breath, leaned back against the desk, and sighed. "So we wait. But listen, kid. Fifteen minutes, he's gotta be here. Sixteen minutes and I'm gone."

T.J. was already out the door. He flew down the steps and outside, then skidded to a stop in front of Kenny Hansen's stand. "Billy!" he called. "Which way'd he go?"

"Billy? Let's see now . . ." Kenny rubbed his chin.

"That way!" Sonny said, pointing.

T.J. ran. Billy had several old haunts in this neighborhood, places he'd visit from time to time, leaving T.J. in the car. He hoped Billy would be in one of them close by.

On the other hand, he hoped he wouldn't, because that would mean . . .

Billy wasn't in either of the first two. Bursting through the door of the third, T.J. saw him. But first he heard him. It wasn't difficult.

Seated behind the drum set and banging away on the tom-toms, Billy slurred some homemade lyrics: "Oh, them Latin senoritas with the flashin' eyes, fell in love 'fore I realize—" Suddenly he stopped and gaped at T.J. Then he pretended to be terrified, cowering behind the drumsticks. "Oooh, look who's here, Luis! Don't let him get me!" He lowered the sticks and sat up straight, now looking stern. "Luis, you better get this child outta here before you lose your license!" He reared back and laughed, downed the last of his drink, then returned to banging the drums. "Pour me another, Luis, and make it a honest double this time!"

T.J. stared at him for a moment, breathing hard. Then he ran over to the bar. "What'll I do?" he asked frantically. "He's gotta be at the gym in a couple a minutes. Mr. Goodman is there! He'll only wait fifteen minutes!" T.J. was shaking.

Luis reached under the bar and brought out a red juice bottle. "Give him this tomato juice," he said, pouring a glass. "And put this ice on his back." He filled another glass with cubes.

T.J. grabbed two cubes in one hand, the tomato juice glass in the other, and hurried over to Billy.

"Hey, what I got here?" Billy straightened up and blinked. "Got me a little mother!" He screwed up his face and spoke in a whining little-boy voice. "Don't do this, Champ, don't do that! Gee whiz, Champ, you spent all your money, Champ!"

T.J. quickly put the ice cubes to the back of Billy's neck, and brought the juice glass close to his lips.

"What the hell—" Reacting to the ice, Billy elbowed T.J.'s arm, knocking the juice glass to the floor where it spattered into red shards.

Luis came out to mop up.

"Can ya stand up, Champ?" T.J. tried desperately to lift him under his arms. "C'mon, Champ, try!"

Billy pushed him away. "Wait a minute, wait a minute."

"But, but we only got—"

"Hush! Stop it, now." He looked off across the room. "Damnedest thing. Driving over here I get this cramp, right down here in my gut." He jabbed at his belly with a forefinger. "Like a knife. I figure it was something I ate, y'know?"

"Those franks and beans at lunch," T.J. said, fighting back tears. "That was probably what it was, Champ. But Mr. Goodman—"

" 'Xactly. Lunch. So I feel this cramp, and I says to myself, 'Whoa, boy, what if the guy taps you in the gut juss once back there and down you go, right in front of Goodman and everbody? How's that gonna look, huh?' " He smiled crookedly at T.J. "So I figure, don't wanna toss away seventy-five grand over a can of franks and beans, by lookin' bad in the ring. Better postpone things." Billy chuckled, then turned serious. "How's Goodman? He mad?"

"He's not mad," T.J. said, shaking his head briskly. "He said you were a great fighter. But he wasn't gonna wait more'n—"

"I figure in a week or so," Billy mused, blinking his unfocused eyes, "when I feel juss right, I go up there and pull on the gloves. Don't say nothing to nobody beforehand. Juss show up and do it. When *I'm* ready, like it should be. Way it oughta be. When the *Champ* is ready. It's *me* gotta do the fighting."

Suddenly he slammed the sticks down on the drums. "It's *me* gotta take the damn punches to this damn headache a mine!"

"Take it easy, Champ." T.J. quickly brushed a tear off his cheek with the back of his hand. "Everything's okay."

Georgie and Hesh came in, nodded to Luis, and came directly over to Billy and T.J.

"I got the car out front, T.J.," Hesh said. "We'll give you a hand."

He and Georgie went to either side of Billy and started to lift him under his arms. Billy staggered against the drum set, knocking over the cymbal with a clang.

"Oh, the head." Billy righted himself, closing his eyes, as they helped him down from the bandstand. "First the stomach, now the head." He put a hand to each spot.

"Goodman waiting?" T.J. asked softly of Georgie.

Georgie shook his head. "Come on, Billy, just lean on us."

"We gotta get back and get some sleep, Champ," T.J. said, taking Billy's hand. "You got roadwork tomorrow, you said."

"Right. Gotta do four miles tomorrow."

"Easy, Billy, car's right outside." Hesh maneuvered him toward the door, Georgie going ahead to open it.

Billy pulled away. "Gotta go to the can."

"I got him," T.J. said, taking his arm to lead him toward the small hallway in the back. "Hang on, Champ."

The two men watched Billy and T.J. disappear into the back, then sat down at the bar. "Two beers, Luis," Hesh said.

Sounds of Billy's vomiting reached the bar. The men grimaced.

"There he goes," Georgie said sadly.

Hesh nodded grimly. "Georgie, what really happened that night?"

"What night?"

"The night he lost the title. He never really explained it."

"I dunno." Georgie's wizened features hardened in a frown. "I just don't know."

They sipped their beer.

"Everybody I ever talked to says Billy threw it away," Hesh said.

Georgie shrugged. He slid his glass in small circles on the bar, spreading the moisture into a glistening oval. "I seen what happened. I ain't sure why it happened." He scratched his ear. "It's like, well, all of a sudden his heart ain't in it."

"Heart!" Hesh grunted. "Nobody had more heart than Billy."

"Yeah."

"He's defending the title." Hesh swiveled to look at Georgie. "How can his heart not be in it?"

Georgie squinted, as if the memory were difficult. "In the sixth he goes out sluggin', you know? No jabbin', no movin', just sluggin'. Like 'you take me out or I take you out, either way it don't matter.'"

"Some kinda suicide or somethin'."

They heard more retching, and T.J.'s comforting voice.

"Caught with a right," Georgie said, shaking his head in disbelief. "Can you believe that, Billy nailed by a damn *right*?"

"And with a left hook like he's got—*nobody* beats him with a sucker right, 'cause they know they're gonna get tagged."

"Yeah. But he takes the right. Then come the punches to his head—up, down, side to side. Every time Billy starts to fall, a punch brings him back up. I wanted to stop it, but . . ." His voice trailed off and he shook his head.

Luis leaned over the bar between them. "Very strange. A man does a thing like that with no reason. 'Specially a fighter, gettin' hurt like that. Lets it happen."

All three men looked down at the bar.

"Jackie said somethin' once," Georgie said. "Or maybe it's a rumor, I ain't sure which, but I heard he said it to some people up there in Chicago later." Luis and Hesh looked at him. Georgie stared straight ahead. "Something to do with the wife. The kid's mother. Somethin' about—"

"It's all right now, Champ." T.J. led Billy up behind them, one arm around his father's waist, letting him lean on his small shoulder with his elbow. "We'll get home, so everything'll be okay."

The three of them helped him out to the Cadillac and into the back seat. T.J. crawled in beside him. Hesh and Georgie got in front, Hesh behind the wheel.

Billy closed his eyes immediately and sank against T.J.

They drove for a few minutes before Georgie turned to the back. "How's he doin'?"

"Sleeping real good," T.J. said softly. "He's okay. He's just . . . he's just been pushing himself too hard lately."

"Yeah." Georgie faced front.

"Marty Casey," Hesh said in a low voice. "You remember Marty Casey?"

"Yeah."

"Marty took a beating the last time out. He don't have the heart for it no more either. He even goes near a gym, he throws up. It's like a bullfighter. The horns get to him one day, he can't forget."

"Like in that Tyrone Power movie."

"Huh?"

"Tyrone Power, you know."

Hesh turned on the radio and fiddled with the dial, bringing in some country music low. He tapped the steering wheel to the rhythm of Mel Tillis. "You got nothin' but the Spanish and blacks now," he said softly. "No white boys want the pain. So much money around for athletes. Baseball, for instance. Guys get a million bucks for standin' around the grass on Sunday afternoon. Why get the face busted?"

Billy's head lolled against T.J., but now his eyes were open, fixed on the back of Hesh's head.

"A fortune in cash," Hesh went on, "just waiting for a good white fighter. I ain't no more prejudiced than Billy there, but a lotta fight fans are, and that's the plain truth—Great White Hope is what they want."

"I *think* it was Tyrone Power," Georgie said. "Good lookin' guy, black hair—"

"White guy. That's the ticket. White fighter who ain't afraid. Sometimes I think we got one, sometimes I think we haven't." He cocked his head toward the back. "Awful high price you gotta pay these days."

Georgie blinked as if waking up. He turned to Hesh. "Price is the same as always, for takin' a punch."

"Yeah, I guess. Then the age, you gotta consider that."

"Age is in the mind," Georgie said, "just like everything else."

"I guess so. So far it don't look so good."

"Nope."

In the back, the wind blew the blond hair of Billy and T.J., and they both closed their eyes.

* * *

At the backstretch, quiet now and dark except for a single floodlight high on a pole, the three of them eased Billy out of the car.

"It's okay," T.J. said, "I got him."

"Sure you don't want some help?" Hesh asked. "He's a lot of man for you to handle."

"No, I got him. It's okay." T.J. steered Billy away from the car and toward the stairs.

"Up to you, T.J."

They drove off, and T.J. urged his weight against Billy, who staggered.

"Couple lousy beers," Billy mumbled, his head drooping. His feet crossed and he stumbled.

T.J. struggled to keep him moving ahead. "It's okay now, Champ. We're home. Everything's okay."

As they neared the wooden stairs leading up to their room, Josie appeared from the shadows. "He okay?" she asked, pulling her robe tightly around her. "Want some help?"

"I'm fine," Billy said in a thick, hoarse voice, "juss fine. Four lousy beers . . ." He yanked T.J. to a stop. "How you, Josie?"

"It was Charlie Goodman's idea," T.J. put in quickly, leaning hard against Billy's tottering form. "Just a couple beers. Everybody was buying the Champ drinks, you know? And . . . and he don't, uh—"

"He doesn't want to hurt their feelings," Josie said. "Right?"

T.J. nodded quickly. "They want him to sign autographs, take pictures, everything, you know—"

"Not it at all!" Billy waved his arms as if signaling time out. "I don't wait for nobody! He held up a finger. "But I'm okay, see? I'm awright."

Josie moved to his other side and took his arm. "Come on, Billy, we'll get you upstairs."

"No, please, Josie, let me do it."

"Okay, T.J." She looked warily at Billy. "I understand. See you in the morning."

"Right." T.J. moved Billy forward again. "And Josie?"

"Yeah?"

"Thanks."

She smiled and turned back toward her room.

It wasn't the first time T.J. had managed to get Billy up the steps this way. He had developed a skill at it. He knew Billy would resist being helped up, and that it mattered to him how it looked, so T.J. stepped aside and allowed Billy to take the steps himself, at his own pace. T.J.'s role here was just to stay close enough to keep Billy from falling.

At length they reached the top and bumped through the screen door. Then Billy lurched forward to flop down on his bed. For a few seconds he lay face down, as if out cold. Then he turned over and put his forearm over his eyes.

"How's the head, Champ?" T.J. asked, leaning over him. "Headache?"

"Naw. Head's fine. I'm hot. Jesus, it's hot in here."

T.J. reached up to switch on the small fan on the shelf, turning it so that the breeze was directed on Billy.

"Don't forget to brush your teeth."

"I won't, Champ."

"Now, so you don't forget."

"Sure, Champ." T.J. went into the bathroom cubicle and turned on the cold water to let it run.

"Do 'em good. Use that fluoride stuff."

"I will. Don't worry."

"Hell, I ain't worried. Nothin' to worry about."

T.J. brushed his teeth noisily, so the Champ could hear. Smells and sounds of the horses filtered into the room. He finished and came over to Billy's bed. "Lemme get your shoes off, Champ." He lifted one leg and pulled at the boot. It was hard to get it off. Little by little he worked it loose.

"All of 'em," Billy said, "Georgie, Hesh, Goodman, now they think I'm yellow, got no guts."

"None of 'em knows shit, Champ."

"Hey! Don't talk like that!" Billy raised his head, winced, and lay back down. "You been taught better."

"Sorry, Champ." He finally got the boot off and dropped it on the floor.

"Anyway, you're right. Don't ever let anybody tell you different. Your old man's got heart."

T.J. nodded. "Champ, you wanna lift the other leg?"

Billy held his foot up and T.J. yanked at the boot.

"None of 'em been in the ring like I have. What can they know?"

"Right, Champ. *Nobody* knows what you know. I ain't never gonna know as much as you."

"Don't say ain't. Anyway, you'll know." He reached out blindly for T.J.'s hair, missed it, let his arm flop back down. "You'll know."

"If I ever know *half* of what you know, Champ, I'll be proud."

Billy chuckled. "Proud. Yeah, that'd be something. Something for my kid."

"I *am* proud—already, I mean."

"Yeah."

T.J. got the second boot off and reached for Billy's belt. "Just let me—"

"Whoa, boy." Billy pushed his hand away and, with difficulty, sat up. "Just hold off on that." He swung his legs off the side of the bed and stood up, wavering a bit before getting his balance. "The day a man can't take off his own pants," he said, unbuckling himself, "he ain't a man."

"Right, Champ."

"Get yourself to bed. It's late."

Billy dropped his pants, stepped out of them, and sank back onto the bed. T.J. removed his own pants, took from his pockets a few coins, an old stopwatch, and a pocketknife, and put them on the dresser. He carefully draped his pants over a chair back and did the same with Billy's. He turned to look at Billy, saw his eyes were closed, and switched off the light.

He lay down quietly, trying to keep the old springs from squeaking. He listened to Billy's steady, deep breathing, then closed his eyes. Despite the fan, the room was stifling. T.J. didn't sweat like his father, but he wished he did.

"No more booze." Billy's voice caused T.J.'s eyes to pop open. "Absolutely no more booze. You got my word on that."

T.J. was silent.

"You hear me?"

"I heard, Champ. No more booze."

"Right. Same goes for gambling. No dice, not even poker in the back of the barn."

T.J. didn't answer.

"You hear me? I mean it."

For a moment T.J. was quiet. Then he said, "Night, Champ."

"Night, T.J."

A radio was playing somewhere, quiet nighttime rock. The air from the fan stirred Billy's hair lightly. His eyes were open. He lay that way for a long time, feeling the heat and the air of the fan, and listening to the distant music and the nearer sleep-breathing of his son.

Billy tried to think. His mind was muddled. It seemed that so many of the things he did were things he shouldn't do. But they were things he somehow *had* to do. Like fighting. He knew that as a fighter he was considered simple by some people. Lawyers and doctors and even horse trainers were not simple. But fighters were. Pugs, they were. But Billy did not think his life was simple. Nothing simple about it. It was complicated and confusing. People thought it was easy when he was Champ. "You got everything anybody could want," they would say. But it was not that simple, even then. They didn't know. Nobody who hadn't been in the ring, taking and giving punches, could know anything about how complicated it was. When you weren't getting hurt, you were hurting somebody else, that was the name of it. Nothing simple about that. Not even fighters talked much about that, or even thought about it. It was too complicated, too difficult to explain or understand.

"A rough way to make a living," people said. Rougher than any of them could ever know. Because you couldn't even explain the feeling a fighter had when he was in the ring and thousands of people were screaming and waving their fists and wanting either one of them to get their brains knocked out.

And because fighters couldn't explain it, it was generally assumed that their brains got scrambled along the way—even the best of them—if they had any brains to begin with. And because people thought that and said that, fighters had to believe it a little.

The problem was, Billy thought, that a fighter never really knew if his brains had got scrambled or not. How can you tell?

He twisted onto his side and looked across to T.J.'s bed, where his son, his small body covering only half the bed, was sleeping. His son was proud of him. But there were some things he didn't want even his son to know. Because he didn't want his son to worry or be afraid. He wanted his son to be strong, and he *was* strong. He was proud of his son. T.J. was gonna be okay.

But he had to make it too, himself. He sat up and blinked hard, trying to clear his head. He was not as drunk now. He squinted in the darkness. Faint light from the moon made the room dimly visible.

He swung his legs off the bed and sat for a few minutes. Then he slowly stood up, staggering a bit at first. He went over to the chair and fished in his pants for his wallet. He opened it, slid a finger into the bill section, found the wallet empty. He picked up his watch from the dresser and peered at it. He couldn't see the hands.

He stood for some moments, staring at nothing, pursing his lips. Then he went over near the window, squatted, pulled up a corner of the tattered rug, and felt along the floorboards.

It didn't take long to find the loose one, and he carefully pulled it up, glancing over to see that T.J. had not moved. He reached under the board, felt around, and took out a small rectangular picture which he held up to the moonlight.

It was a yellowing Polaroid photograph of T.J. on a horse. Billy studied it. He had looked at that photograph many times, but not since T.J. had put it away in what was supposed to be a secret hiding place. It was a picture Josie had taken, and for a while Billy just looked at it, enjoying the recollection. It was as if the time were brought back. T.J. sitting on that fine young racehorse, so tiny on its bare back, glowing with pleasure and pride, trying to look grown-up. Billy remembered how nervous he was while T.J. was sitting there, because those horses are so high-strung. But he had encouraged T.J. to get on, to make them both proud. T.J. had wanted to get on the horse, but was a little afraid until his father said it was okay.

He put the photograph back in its place and took out a cigar box. He opened it to find a single twenty dollar bill. He looked over at T.J., who still had not moved. He plucked out the bill, replaced the floorboard, and smoothed the rug over it. He quickly pulled on his pants and boots, stuffed the bill into a pocket, and tiptoed from the room.

He was not exactly ashamed of what he was doing. Because it was a hopeful act. The hope was faint, to be sure, but when is hope not?

CHAPTER 3

The gambling room, hidden over a dance floor, was easy to get into, but it was hard to leave.

Billy had not been there long—twenty dollars does not have great longevity. He put his last single on the table, fervently blew on the dice in his hand, and rolled them out.

"Seven—a loser," droned the stickman as he raked in the dice. "Next shooter."

Billy stepped back, his hands shaking slightly. He took a fifty-cent piece out of his otherwise empty pockets and flipped it lightly. He looked around at the other crap tables, the roulette wheel, the card layouts, all crowded with players. Most were well dressed—better, at least, than he. But nobody noticed him. Everyone's attention was fastened on the games. This was not a social gathering.

He listened to the babble of voices rising and falling around him, the whispers of excitement, the groans of loss, the labored hopefulness of going against the odds.

Against one wall was a line of slot machines. Tossing the coin in his hand, he walked past the dime machines and quarter machines to stand in front of the three fifty-cent machines. Silently he tried to guess which machine to play. He decided on the one to his left and started to drop the coin in.

"Not that one, mister," said a man in a sport jacket

and open shirt, carrying a handful of coins. "You don't want to play that one."

"What's the problem?" Billy asked, taking the coin out of the slot.

"Problem is," the man said quietly, leaning toward him, "someone just hit the jackpot on that one five minutes ago. Lightning doesn't hit twice in a row, friend."

"Thanks," Billy said, nodding. "Appreciate it."

The man waved and moved off.

Billy studied the two remaining machines. He decided on the one on the right just as a birdlike old woman stepped up to the one he had abandoned. She dropped her coin in before he could warn her off.

She pulled the crank; the fruits spun, then clanked to a stop. Coins clattered out the chute. "Jackpot!" she hollered, holding out her hat to catch some of the tumbling coins. "Jackpot!" Coins continued to cascade from the machine and roll on the floor around her.

Billy gaped, stunned, as she stooped to gather the tide of money. Other people knelt beside her to help, picking up coins and dumping them into her hat. He was still holding his fifty-cent piece when the woman rose, snatched the coin from his fingers, and said, "Thank you."

"Forgive me, lady," Billy said, grabbing it back, "that's *mine*."

"Really?" She eyed him haughtily, as if he were a petty thief.

"Really. Now get the hell out of my way."

She stepped grudgingly aside, nodding at the people standing around.

Billy stepped to the middle machine, looked at it and at the coin, contemplated the other two machines, then finally raised the coin dramatically. Closing his eyes, the better to see faint hope, he dropped the coin into the slot and pulled the crank.

THE CHAMP

* * *

It was noon on the backstretch. Morning chores were over, afternoon ones in the offing. The regulars were gathered in a loose circle under some shading palms, chatting, nodding, just taking it easy. Beau half-dozed in his favorite canvas chair. Josie and a couple of younger girls rubbed saddle soap into pieces of tack. A teenage apprentice jockey named Jeffy skimmed the latest issue of *Newsweek*. T.J. sat astride a feed bucket, tilting forth and back, mostly listening to the grown-ups talking around him.

The talk turned to Billy. "How'd it go yesterday?" Josie asked. "I mean, before the, uh, celebration."

"Fine," T.J. said cheerily. "You know, Goodman offered him a deal, you know."

"What kind of deal?" Beau asked, suddenly sitting up straight.

"Oh, you know, regular deal. So the Champ tells Goodman straight off, TV rights or no fight."

"That a fact?" Beau settled back and closed his eyes again.

Josie studied her hands. T.J. reached down to pluck some blades of grass and tossed them off, watching them float back to the ground.

"Where is Billy anyway?" Jeffy asked, closing his magazine and lying back on the hay bale with his hands clasped behind his head.

"Champ says fifty grand for TV," T.J. went on quickly. "He don't sign for a nickel less."

"But where is—"

"Goodman says he's gotta think it over." T.J. looked around at all the faces, his eyes wide and innocent. "The Champ says go ahead and think, but—"

Billy's Caddy roared into the backstretch, the engine loud through its decaying muffler.

"He better get that fixed," Beau said, not moving.

T.J. bounced off the feed bucket and ran over to the car.

Dust boiled up around Billy as he slumped behind the wheel, looking dejected and exhausted.

"Where ya been, Champ?" T.J. whispered urgently. "I been goin' *nuts!*"

Billy slid wearily out of the car and leaned back against it. "Nuts? Everybody's nuts. You been goin' nuts because your old man is nuts, so you got it in your blood." He smiled down at T.J.'s anxious face. "So don't worry about it." He mussed T.J.'s hair.

"But, but—"

Billy walked away from him, toward the circle of his friends.

"Missed your work, Billy," Beau said without looking up.

"I know, sorry. What can I do?" Billy spread his arms humbly and hunched his shoulders. "I'm nuts."

T.J. stood off to one side looking at Billy, trying to figure out what it meant, Billy's being away all morning and everything, and how he seemed to be trying to make a joke out of it.

"It's okay anyway," Josie said. "Everything's done."

"Well, I owe you," Billy said, leaning over to tap her shoulder. Then he straightened up and paced around among them, scratching his head as if trying to figure something out. "Can't sleep last night, you know? Around eleven thirty, twelve, something like that, I'm layin' there thinking. I think, 'Damn, damn, you did it again, blew every last buck on booze. That's an unforgivable sin.'"

They looked away and fidgeted as Billy nodded at them.

"An unforgivable sin," he repeated.

"How many times I tell you, Billy?" Beau said. "You go out there, nobody gives a damn, nobody's your friend." The old man waved a hand around at the circle. "Here you got friends. Go out from the backstretch, what you get?"

"Fifteen tons less horse manure for starters," Josie said, trying to lighten things.

"A rotten sin," Billy said, ignoring her and Beau, "that's what it was!" He slapped his thigh and stomped around. "Then I steal twenty bucks from my kid—" T.J. blinked "—and like some dummy I drive out to Oscar's, figure I can run it up."

Nobody looked up from the circle; eyes were averted in embarrassment at these revelations. Even T.J. now looked away, wishing his father wouldn't tell all this.

But Billy continued, almost eagerly. "Five minutes at the crap table," he said, gesturing as if rolling dice, "and I'm down to my last lousy paper buck. Then just one more roll—that's gone too. What I got left? I got fifty cents. That's right. One shiny half-dollar."

"You lose the fifty cents too, Billy?" Beau said, snorting.

"A sin!" Billy spread his arms, his eyes sloping in sorrow, beseeching the people around him. "I tell ya, it was a sin!"

"We heard that," Beau said, crossing his legs, folding his arms, and closing his eyes.

"I stole from my own kid!"

"It don't matter, Champ." T.J. darted forward to touch his arm. "Honest, it don't matter!"

Billy stepped over in front of Beau and looked down sadly. "Beau, you're a holy man in my book. Bless me or something, take this stain off me."

Beau opened his eyes a little, looked askance at Billy, then eased out of his chair and slipped off to the side, as if afraid of being touched by this strange man.

"Beau, where ya going? Let me rub your head or

something. Don't that bring luck or something like that?"

"Nowhere, Billy." Beau eyed him uneasily. "Just ease up, I ain't goin' nowhere."

T.J. tugged lightly at Billy's shirt. "It's okay, Champ," he said in a shaking voice. "The money was for both of us. It was okay to use it. Just bad luck, Champ. I don't mind!"

Suddenly Billy stopped and leaned back and emitted a low, wicked laugh. "Take the lousy half buck, toss it in the slot"—he waved a fist in the air triumphantly—"and *whammo*! Bells, plums, cherries show up, then halves pour outta that chute for five minutes!"

At once all heads turned toward him, mouths fell open, eyes widened.

"That's right! Jackpot!" Billy grinned and held both fists in front of him. Beau slid back into his chair. T.J. looked up at Billy in wonder.

Billy crouched, looking at each of them. He lowered his voice dramatically. "Then I hit the crap table again. I get them dice and people start screaming 'cause I make seven straight passes lettin' it ride every time." His voice crescendoed. "And when I walk out I got sixty-four hundred bucks shoved in my pockets!"

Billy beamed at the shocked faces, letting his words register. "It's a fact! Sixty-four hundred bucks!" He watched as they mouthed the figure silently. "You know how much bread that is? Hey!" Again he spread his arms grandly, palms lifted skyward, and tilted back his head. "The Lord works in strange ways, but damn, He works!"

Nobody made a sound.

"Yeah, I know. You're wondering, did I blow it all? Did I stay at the table until my luck turned bad again? Did I, huh?" He gave them a pretended scowl. "Am

I that dumb, huh? Well, the answer is no, I am not that dumb. Come over here, everybody, and take a look!"

There were some initial gasps, then chuckles, then laughs, and they followed Billy over to his car. He held his arms above the car as if pronouncing benediction. The seats were loaded with gifts. "Santa Claus time!" he crowed.

Before Billy could reach into the car, T.J. jumped on his back, hugging him with arms and legs. "Never count out the Champ! The Champ always comes through!"

Billy plucked him off his back and hugged him. "Yes sir, Santa Claus time! And here we go!" He put T.J. down, slapped his rear, and reached over the door to begin passing out packages. The first was in pink paper, beautifully wrapped with a pink ribbon. He tossed it to Josie. "Something sexy for a very sexy lady," he said as she blushed. "I suggest you try it on in private." Billy blew her a kiss and she blew one back.

"Maybe she try it on for you, Billy," Beau said with a knowing smile.

"And Donna Mae"—he held out a small package to the girl—"here's something to make you smell as good as you look."

She leaned over to give him a peck on the cheek.

"And Jeffy"—he took out a bag of several magazines—"I know how you always go on about how you like to look at fillies up close. . . ." He tossed the bag to Jeffy, and they spilled out, causing Jeffy to blush deep red. "So there's some pictures of how *girls* look. Read 'em later, kid, not in front of these hot walkers here."

He enjoyed Jeffy's embarrassment as the young jockey tried to stuff the girlie magazines back into the bag. Then he brought out another small package. "Something special for you to smoke, Beau."

Beau caught the package, ripped it open, and held up a pipe. "But you know I don't smoke, Billy."

"I suggest," Billy said with a sly wink, "that you and Jeffy get together and work out some kinda swap for a while."

"Yeah, I could handle that," Beau said, winking at Jeffy, who looked shyly away, holding the magazines tightly under his arm.

Billy tossed out the remaining packages. When there were none left, everybody fell abruptly silent.

Billy looked around at them. "So there you are, everbody. How's that, huh?"

T.J. crawled into the car and perched on the folded-down top, looking at the empty seats.

Josie cleared her throat. "Um, what'd you get for T.J.?"

"Huh?" Billy looked stunned.

"I said—"

"Wait a minute!" Billy clapped a hand to his head and fell back against the Cadillac. "Damn! I don't believe it! T.J.! How could I forget?"

"My oh my," Beau mumbled.

"My own kid! How the hell—my own kid!" Billy shook his head fiercely.

"It ain't important, Champ," T.J. called softly from the car.

Those standing around, who moments before had gleefully accepted their presents, now stood dumbly looking at the ground.

"I feel terrible," Billy groaned, slapping the hood of the car. "I'm a bum, a rotten bum pug!" Slowly he straightened up and turned around toward them. "Wait a sec. Just a minute here." He scratched his head. "Seems to me there *was* something. What was it?"

"It don't matter, Champ, honest," T.J. said.

"I got it! I remember now!" He looked at T.J. out of the corner of his eyes, "Nothin' much, you understand. Wasn't even sure T.J. would want it."

He felt the nervous eyes on him from all his friends of the backstretch. He bit his lip, then cupped a hand beside his mouth and called over his shoulder, "Hey, Mr. Riley? That little something I picked up for T.J., you wanna bring it out here?"

There was a hush, then gasps as from around the corner of the barn came Riley, leading the beautiful copper-toned filly, She's A Lady, her mane and tail festooned with red ribbons and a banner slung over her back reading T.J. FLYNN.

"What the hell are you sittin' there for?" Billy said to the dumbfounded T.J. "If you don't like her I'll take her back!"

T.J. gaped at Billy, then at the horse, then at Billy again. Billy nodded to him. T.J.'s eyes opened even wider. "She's mine? Mine?" Billy nodded again. T.J. sprang off the car, waving his fists. "Mine, all mine! She's A Lady is mine!" He lunged into Billy's arms as the group erupted in cheers.

"Champ! Jeez! I don't—I just . . ."

Billy wiped T.J.'s eyes quickly and pushed him toward the horse. "You don't haveta nothin'. She's yours, that's all there is to it. So quit blubbering and get up on her so's I can see how you look!"

He hoisted his son onto the back of She's A Lady. The group formed a ring around them, and Billy led the horse in a parade, with T.J. leaning forward to pat the filly's neck and shaking his head with the wonder of it all.

The admiring group oohed and aahed and applauded.

"Way to go, T.J.!"

"What a picture! Somebody get a picture!"

"Careful now, watch her, she's high-strung!"

Several hands reached out to tap T.J.'s legs as he passed by.

"Can she race?" T.J. asked. "Huh, Champ, can she race? Can I race her?"

"Can she race! Can birds fly? Of course she'll race! She'll do whatever you say. You're her owner, aren't you?"

Another cheer went up from the circle, and T.J. lay forward over the horse's neck, rubbing it with his cheek, patting it with his hands. Then, as they circled, he reached out and took Billy's hand, and they paraded together.

*   *   *

Hialeah was jammed. It was February, the middle of the best racing season in years. Cars jammed the parking lots, people jammed the entry passages to buy programs and souvenirs; people jammed the grandstand, those in better areas filling the green wicker chairs. The broad stairways hewn from coral rock were jammed too. Pink and white banners flew, and the pink flamingos fluttered and danced and strutted around the ponds in the manicured infield. The large board in the infield facing the grandstand carried the message TRACK FAST—TURF FIRM.

And indeed it was. The mile-and-an-eighth course was raked and wet down, the claylike turf sparkling in the sun.

To the rear of the mighty, multitiered grandstand —where the statue of the great 1948 Triple Crown winner, Citation, rose above the crowd—people wandered among the gardens and pressed up against the parade ring, where horses would soon be led around for inspection and sizing up before the race.

People jammed the betting windows too, up in the back of the grandstand, where they could look down

27

upon the gardens and the royal palms and the parade ring.

And behind that, beyond the chain-link fence, in the paddock area between the grandstand and the backstretch, trainers oversaw carefully the saddling process, clucking to the horses, muttering to the assistants and jockeys, fretting and sweating and worrying. Some horses pawed the ground, some stood still as if bored with the process. Jockeys fretted too, prancing around nervously in their bright silks that were the colors representing the various owning farms.

Monied owners and friends and associates milled around in their finery; others pressed up against the fence to watch the expensive and fragile thoroughbreds being saddled.

Just now the crowd at the fence was watching as a handsome and straight-backed man with salt-and-pepper hair and a blue blazer got his TV crew in position for an interview. Holding the mike and waiting for the cue from his director, he was standing with an elegant elderly woman, well coiffed and well dressed —Dolly Kenyon.

Dolly Kenyon was well-known to the horse crowd. She was, in fact, a grande dame of American turf racing, owner of breeding farms in Kentucky and Ireland. Wealthy beyond most people's dreams, she was as highspirited as her horses, strong, articulate, ambitious, and impatient. She sighed and tapped her cane on the ground while waiting for the questions.

Behind her, just out of camera range, stood a couple of the type the gossip columns usually called "glamorous," Dr. and Mrs. Michael Phillips—he a handsome, graying man in his late forties, she ten years younger, model-thin with a model's high cheekbones. Both of them, like Dolly Kenyon, had a bearing that was at once aristocratic and pleasant. These were people comfortable with their world.

The interviewer got his cue and turned toward his subject with a wide smile. "And here we have Mrs. Dolly Kenyon, owner of the brilliant former champion Justasec."

"Don't forget this race today," Dolly put in brusquely. "I've got a horse in this race too."

"Of course," the man said, not relinquishing his frozen smile. "You mean Dolly's Chance."

"That's right. Number two." She pointed with her cane to a nearby stall. "That little bay there. She didn't cost much, but she's a good animal."

In the stall adjacent to the one to which she pointed stood She's A Lady, with T.J. at her side. T.J. nuzzled and patted his horse as he watched and listened to the TV interview.

"Anyway," Mrs. Kenyon went on, "I like to take chances. Anyone can pay hundreds of thousands of dollars for horses like Justasec. But I don't mind telling you that I paid just next to nothing for Dolly's Chance, and she's going to win this race."

"Well, we certainly appreciate your candid—"

"Baloney!" came T.J.'s voice.

"Who said that?" Dolly commanded, snapping her head around.

"Excuse me?" the TV interviewer asked, looking confused.

"Baloney," Dolly said, "somebody said baloney." She waggled her cane at the stalls. "Who said that?"

"Now, Mrs. Kenyon"—the TV man nipped at her sleeve to get her attention—"you were telling us about—"

"Was that you, little boy?" She glowered over at T.J., who leaned against the stall and tried to look casual. "Was it you?"

"You weren't supposed to hear," he said with chagrin.

"I heard." She stepped toward him, smacking her cane on the ground at each step. "I'm old, but I'm not deaf."

Mike and Annie Phillips, trailing behind the flustered TV man, grasped each other's hands and tried to smother their giggles.

"What about—" The TV man had to clear his voice. "Mrs. Kenyon, what about Dolly's Chance?" He ran out of cord to his mike and was yanked to a stop. He looked desperately at his director, who gave the signal to continue from where he was. "Mrs. Kenyon," he cried, "what about—"

"Dolly's Chance?" She fastened her eyes on T.J. and didn't turn around, giving the camera a view of only her back. "She's just a horse, just a horse. But whatever the, ahem, experts here may say, she's going to win this race!" She stepped directly in front of T.J. and thumped her cane with finality.

"Well, thanks very much," the TV man grumbled. And then, regaining his composure, he waved, smiled into the camera, and said, "And good luck, Mrs. Dolly Kenyon."

"Hmmph." Dolly said. "Sassy little boy, how'd you like your mouth washed out with soap?" Her tone—gentler and tinged with irony—belied the harshness of the words. "And what are you doing here anyway?"

T.J., having been taken by surprise before, summoned his courage. "What do you mean, what am I doing here? I'm a horse-owner like you! And my horse"—he pointed to She's A Lady—"*mine* is gonna win!"

"Your horse?" She quickly assessed the horse. "Hmm. Not a bad-looking filly." She knitted her brows. "But who says she's going to win? Just you?

What are her bloodlines?" She turned slowly and elegantly toward him, arching her eyebrows. "You know anything about bloodlines, boy?"

"Sweet Destruction out of Earth Dancer!"

Some laughter came from nearby, causing T.J. to blush. But Dolly silenced that quickly with a harsh glare at the watching throng. Turning back to him and cocking her head, she said, "What's your name, little boy? Speak up."

"T.J."

"I asked your name, not your initials."

"Look," T.J. said, with growing nervousness about this impressive lady, "I gotta talk to my rider." He began backing away.

"Little smartpants," Dolly muttered, turning and leading her entourage from the stall.

Annie Phillips, drawn by T.J.'s pretended cockiness, his forced manliness, and by his claim to actually own this horse, lingered to listen while T.J. talked to Jeffy.

Jeffy, resplendent in his orange and green silks, etched a small circle in the dirt with his boot as T.J. spoke.

"Don't let her get pushed to the outside, Jeffy."

Jeffy nodded.

"And don't get boxed in."

"I know."

"And don't let her get off the pace too far."

"I know, I *know* all that," Jeffy said irritably. "I'm the damn jockey, for Pete's sake!"

T.J. looked away sheepishly, and his eyes fell on the pretty woman watching him.

She smiled, and T.J. tried to smile back.

"Hi," Annie said. "That really your horse?"

"Yup."

"Nice-looking animal." She took a step toward him. "Very racy, good tone."

"Were you with, you know, that lady? That 'sassy boy wash your mouth out with soap' lady?"

Annie chuckled. "She's a friend of mine. She's really very nice."

"That don't matter." T.J. started to lead his horse out of the stall. "Bet on mine. You'll make a million, believe me." He glanced up at her, trying to look confident.

"Well, I need a million," Annie said, putting a finger to her chin thoughtfully. "But if she doesn't pay off, I'm coming to see you."

"You mean—" T.J. suddenly stopped to look up at her, "you mean you're really going to bet on her, on She's A Lady?"

"You said I'd win."

"You *will*, honest!"

"But if I don't . . ."

"I know, you'll come to see me."

"Right."

"Okay," he said, businesslike. "I'm T.J. Just ask for me. But you'll win."

Annie extended her hand. "I believe you. My name's Annie."

They shook hands, and T.J. led his horse out toward the parade ring.

Emerging into the gardened area behind the grandstand, T.J. became suddenly and uncomfortably aware of all the sights and sounds that surrounded and filled the park. People were wearing dresses and suits and shirts and slacks of various pastels, of which, on the women at least, the predominant shade was pink. There were pink hats and pink ribbons and pink gloves and pink shoes. Off to one side down a shaded walk he caught glimpses of a Cuban steel band playing its captivating, tinny rhythms amid gay people dancing or moving their shoulders or snapping their fingers in time.

All around him people laughed and screeched and milled in dizzying patterns.

He felt very small. He *was*, of course. As small as were the jockeys perched over the necks of the race horses, he was even tinier beneath the neck of She's A Lady as they headed to the parade ring. Jeffy towered over him. People watching from outside the railing towered over him.

In numerical order, the horses were led around the ring. She's A Lady had drawn number one. Jeffy's face was set in concentration.

T.J. was proud but nervous. They had talked about it, he and Billy. Billy had insisted that T.J. was capable of leading his horse around the ring. "You can handle her," Billy had said, "nothin' to worry about."

"But what if I can't?" T.J. had said.

"Hey," Billy had said, tapping a fist gently under T.J.'s chin, "since when does T.J. talk about can't? Would you be the owner of that horse if you couldn't handle her, huh?"

"No," T.J. had answered, hoping it was true.

And then Billy had said, "And I'll be right there nearby to make sure nobody messes with you."

Billy was always right there, all ready to do whatever was necessary to make things go right. T.J. was comforted by that knowledge as he led She's A Lady around. Billy was so strong. T.J. never thought of him as violent—never saw him violent, in fact. But there was a bottom line that Billy owned: If it ever came to it, nobody could stand up to him. Champion of the whole world meant that nobody in the whole world could stand up to him, not when he was there to see that nobody messed with T.J.

He did not look around for Billy, but jabbered up to the silent Jeffy: "Feelin' okay? She feel good? Think she's nervous? You really ready? Pretty hot today, huh? Think the crowd'll bother her? Think she'll go into the gate good, huh, Jeffy?"

But Jeffy was lost in his own preparative thoughts, and just stared at the back of his mount's neck with half-closed eyes.

Annie and Mike Phillips walked toward the Turf Club.

"Was that a kid or a jockey, back there at the stalls?" Mike asked her, chuckling.

"You see Dolly?" Annie shook her head. "She can sure try to sound tough sometimes. Gave the boy a real tough time."

"I think she was flirting with him, if you want the truth. So were you."

She leaned against him and took his hand.

"He really own that horse?" Mike asked.

"Well, he says he does. And he seemed to be in charge, all right. I promised to bet on her."

"What?" He stopped and looked at her.

"I did, I promised. She's A Lady."

"Huh?"

"The name of the horse—She's A Lady. Number one. Do me a favor?"

"Of course."

"Bet on her for me."

"But what about Dolly's—"

"Please? Ten dollars. Just a hunch, but I liked them."

"Them?"

"The horse and the boy. Mostly the boy. Something about him. I mean, so little, and yet so strong somehow. Okay?"

"Sure, okay." He looked doubtful. "See you at the club in a few minutes." He moved away through the throng.

"And Mike?" she called. "Better not mention it to Dolly."

He waved and headed for the betting windows.

The ten-dollar line moved slowly, but Mike, as always, was patient. No matter where, he carried himself with a quiet dignity that made people around him feel confident and secure. He noticed a voice dominating the line next to him.

". . . So what the hell, you know kids, right? He loves horses. So I say, so what, I pick one up. It's running in this race."

He turned slowly to find the source. And when he saw it, he recognized it at once. The faces of boxing champions have a way of sticking with you—especially this one.

Billy was chewing gum furiously as he stood in the next line, prattling to anybody who would listen. "Last year my kid sees this blue Mustang. Nice clean little car. The kid wants that. Seven-year-old kid, he wants a car. Well, you know, nothing I can do about that. So this year it's a horse he wants, so I say okay, horse ain't such a bad idea. I scrape together six grand, pick up a horse. He's nuts about it. You want to see a sight, oh jeez, that is a sight to see. Him and that horse." Billy stopped his monologue just long enough to place his bet. When he reached the window, he slapped down a bill and said loudly, "Gimme Number One ten times."

Mike watched him, then found himself at his window. "Oh, uh, one ticket on Number One."

The teller leaned forward. "Can't hear ya, mister."

"Sorry. One ticket on Number One, please."

He got his ticket and turned quickly back to the adjacent line, but Billy was already gone.

* * *

The horses were being led from the parade ring along the path of rubberlike artificial turf, through the tunnel under the grandstand, toward the track. The frisky, nervous thoroughbreds were escorted by lead ponies on their flanks. Jockeys, their feet high in the stirrups, bowed over their mounts as if in prayer—which was not far from the fact. They were concentrating on their jobs, on the precise strategy, timing, rhythm their upcoming rides would demand. Each knew his horse well, how it would respond to slight shifts in weight, pressure, voice, heels, and slaps of the whip.

Donna Mae, aboard a swaybacked pinto, escorted Jeffy on She's A Lady, clucking occasionally to the inexperienced racehorse. Billy and T.J. walked alongside, never taking their eyes off their charge.

"Just don't force her off the pace," Billy said. "Keep her in tight, watch for an opening."

"Look," Jeffy said with quiet exasperation, "quit tellin' me how to ride my race."

The horse shied for a moment, and Donna Mae nudged her pinto against it to keep it in line.

"Don't let 'em box you in," Billy continued.

Jeffy shifted in the small saddle. "Quit bugging me. I'll find daylight."

"Buggin' you?" Billy frowned. "Who in blazes are you, Jeffy? You ain't Shoemaker or Cauthen. Come on, this is your first race. You gotta listen up."

"I already listened all I can," Jeffy said, glancing down at him. "I gotta think about the race. Don't worry, I got it down."

"Hey, I ain't worried," Billy smiled, trying to ease things by patting the jockey's knee. "You'll do just fine, just great. We got a lot of confidence in you."

Billy knew the jockey was right—there is a time just before competition when further instruction is disruptive, disturbs the concentration of the competitor. It was the same thing in the ring. In the final moments before the opening bell, what the fighter needed was encouragement. He already knew all he was going to know about his own skills and job. "You're gonna be super out there, Jeffy. We're proud to have you up."

In truth, Billy worried a little about Jeffy's competence. He had plenty of natural skill and had trained hard, but he was inexperienced. At first, Billy had suggested that for She's A Lady's first race they should choose a jock with some races under his belt. But T.J. had wanted Jeffy, his friend from the backstretch, and Riley okayed it. And it was fine with Billy. He had really meant it: This was T.J.'s horse, T.J.'s race. Jeffy would be okay.

T.J., having babbled incessantly in the parade ring, was now silent as he walked alongside. Thoughts, fears, doubts, expectations tumbled together in his brain, creating a jumble of notions that left him silent. He gently tapped his horse's damp flank. "Good girl," he said to himself.

Over the loudspeaker came the trumpeted "Last call to the post." Billy and T.J. left the horse to the track handlers who would maneuver her into the starting gate, and headed for the grandstand.

"Don't force her off the pace," Billy called to Jeffy, unable to resist a parting shot of advice.

The horses moved up behind the gate in a drawn-out line, dancing and shaking their heads in a nervous sweat.

In the Turf Club overlooking the track, Dolly Kenyon sat with Annie Phillips. White-jacketed waiters scurried around delivering last-minute drinks to the boisterous crowd of "beautiful people," the rich and energetic stars of horse racing's social whirl. The windows of the club afforded a panoramic view of the oval track, and within the track the ponds and exotic birds. Beyond the track, the feathery branches of the towering Australian pines wafted in a slight breeze.

A black waiter bowed to Dolly and excused himself

for interrupting. "Just want you to know the boy's leg is fine now, thanks to you, Mrs. Kenyon." His son had been hospitalized with a broken ankle, and Dolly had taken care of everything. "You're a very special lady."

"Oh, cut the bull, Johnny. Glad he's doing well. You go on now"—she fluttered a hand impatiently —"and get me another Scotch. Bring it to me near the window."

They started for the window when Mike arrived. He handed the ticket to Annie.

"What'd you bet?" Dolly asked, looking down on the track.

"One," Mike said absently.

"One?"

"He means one ticket," Annie said, examining her husband's look.

"Hmmph, you're a regular big-time gambler," Dolly said. "I would have thought you'd spring for something respectable for Dolly's Chance."

Annie took her husband's hand. "What's wrong, Mike?"

"Hmm?"

"What's the matter? You're not here."

"No, no, nothing." He smiled and squeezed her hand. "Everything's fine." He avoided her eyes. "I forgot to tell you, they rescheduled the lecture for the thirteenth."

"So? You're not superstitious. That's not what's wrong."

"Really, everything's fine." Now he smiled at her. "Really. Just something I ran across. Tell you after the race."

They elbowed in beside Dolly at the windows.

The track announcer boomed over the PA: "The horses are on the track for the first race at six furlongs . . ."

Hoisting T.J. ahead of him, Billy pushed furiously through the crowd. "Excuse me . . . pardon me . . . sorry, ma'am . . . owner coming through . . ."

They reached the rail and T.J. hopped down. "Is she okay? Is she actin' good, Champ?" T.J. asked.

"Perfect, she's in perfect shape, T.J."

T.J. clambered up on the rail to see better.

The horses were prodded toward the stalls of the starting gate. They pranced and tossed their heads. Handlers pushed at their flanks and headed them in. One horse reared, almost throwing its rider, but the handlers quickly calmed it down, maneuvered it forward, and shut the rear gate behind it.

She's A Lady went in smoothly, to Jeffy's great relief. Jittery horses knocked against the sides of the gates, working their lips around the bits. All the jockeys sat poised in their saddles.

The starter watched closely.

"The horses are all in the gate," said the announcer. "The flag is up . . ."

The starter dipped his flag and the gate snapped open explosively; the horses lunged as one out of the gate.

". . . and they're off and running!"

The crowd roared, the din drowning out the thundering hooves. Tightly bunched at first, the horses fanned out for position around the near turn.

T.J. bounced up and down. "C'mon, baby!" he yelled, waving his fist. "That's it! Hold her right there!"

"Right where we want her!" Billy shouted. "Not too much head, Jeffy!"

The galloping racers flashed like polished bronze in the sun, turf spraying under their hooves like hundreds of tiny, distant bomb blasts.

"Dolly's Chance by a length," intoned the track announcer. "Then it's Steel Beauty, TT's Baby one back.

Moving up hard on the outside is She's A Lady, and it's Wartime, then well back it's Manstopper . . ."

"All out, right now!" Billy yelled. "All out! Let out the gas!"

"C'mon, Jeffy!" T.J. hollered at the same time. "Move her! Move her!"

"Set her down, Jeffy! Set her down!"

The crowd surged in around them. Billy elbowed people away to keep T.J.'s line of sight clear. "*Now,* Jeffy!"

". . . Dolly's Chance, with She's A Lady closing fast," came the call as the horses swept into the back straight. "Wartime three back . . ."

"She's A Lady, She's A Lady!" chanted Billy and T.J. together as they bounced up and down.

"Dolly's Chance, Dolly's Chance," urged Dolly Kenyon high behind the Turf Club glass, watching the race through binoculars.

"C'mon Number One!" called Annie.

"She's Number Two, for heaven's sake," Dolly growled.

"C'mon Number One!"

"Who in blazes are you pulling for, Annie?"

". . . Nearing the sixteenth pole, it's Dolly's Chance by a neck over She's A Lady . . . Wartime moving up on the outside, closing to half a length—"

It happened in the blink of an eye: She went down between horses, Jeffy cartwheeling over her head. The crowd hushed instantly as the rest of the field churned by the fallen horse and rider, the hooves slicing dangerously to either side as jockeys tried to check their mounts. Jeffy huddled beside his horse, then sprang to his feet.

"She's down!" T.J. gasped, struggling in Billy's arms.

"No, no!" Shock stiffened Billy's face.

"She's hurt! Please, God . . ." T.J. tried to wrest free.

"It's all right, T.J.! Hold it! Listen to me! She's gonna . . ."

But T.J. broke free, hurtled the rail, and dashed onto the track. Billy came right behind him.

At the same time, the announcer called the end of the race: "At the finish it's Dolly's Chance by three lengths over Wartime. Number One, She's A Lady, is the horse that went down."

Annie's hands shook holding the binoculars. "Dammit, no! It's the boy's horse!"

She's A Lady was now on her feet, but hobbling badly. Jeffy, shaken but unhurt, grabbed for the frightened horse's reins. "Easy, girl! Take it easy! Damn! Okay, easy, babe!"

T.J. ran up, tears pouring down his cheeks, his voice choked. "No, no! Her leg's broke!"

"I kill myself!" Jeffy hauled in on the reins. "Anything happens to her, I kill myself!"

"It wasn't your fault!" Billy shouted, trying to grab T.J.'s shoulders.

But T.J. sank to his knees near the horse's game leg. "It's broke!" he sobbed. "They're gonna shoot her! They're gonna shoot my She's A Lady because her leg's broke!"

Billy dropped to his own knees beside T.J., putting an arm around him tightly.

The crowd, still on its feet, focused on the scene, people talking in fearful whispers that sounded like the wind.

She's A Lady stumbled, dancing toward T.J. on three legs. Billy pulled T.J. to his feet and back, T.J. still fighting to be near his horse.

"Okay, T.J., it's okay. Just gotta get out from under her hooves, that's all."

T.J.'s whole body shook from shock and sobs.

Annie slowly lowered the binoculars from her eyes.

"Mike, it's Billy. That's Billy out there, down there with that boy."

Mike nodded soberly. "Yes, I know. I was going to tell you—"

"Dammit," Dolly muttered, "it's that cheeky boy's horse, all right. Damned sad." She turned to them. "What are you two mumbling about? What's going on here? Will somebody answer my questions?"

Annie again brought the binoculars to her eyes, holding them as steadily as she could with her quivering hands. "Is he Timmy?" she asked softly. "Mike? Is he? The boy who calls himself T.J.?"

Mike swallowed hard. "I don't know." He thought so, but wasn't sure.

Annie abruptly turned and started away. Mike grabbed for her arm. "Wait a minute Annie, please . . ."

She wheeled around, fixing him for a moment with sad eyes.

"Okay." He knew her look. It meant for him to stay. He understood how hard it had suddenly become for her. "I'll be here."

She left the club almost at a run.

CHAPTER 4

Doc ran a hand through his gray hair, then wiped it on his white coat. He removed his glasses and passed a handkerchief over his sweating forehead. He put his glasses back on and squatted again beside She's A Lady. Again he traced the bone under the fetlock with his fingers, gently probing the horse's delicate leg.

Those watching in Barn Eleven on the backstretch were somber and still, as if to move or speak might break the spell of silence and cause Doc to make the pronouncement they all dreaded. Doc was silent, they were silent. Beau, Josie, Donna Mae, Jeffy, and others watched with eyes leadened in grief and apprehension.

But their grief was nothing compared to the inconsolable anguish felt by T.J. Billy's arms encircled him from the rear, and he tried to hold his head up, tried to stem the tears, tried to be tall. She's A Lady stood tall before him—proudly, T.J. thought. Once in a while his horse snorted, and T.J. felt the hard lump in his throat threaten to gag him. His horse was in pain, and there was nothing he could do, nothing he could explain to She's A Lady, nothing he could set right.

For the briefest part of an instant, T.J. wished it had never happened, none of it—that Billy had never gambled and won and bought gifts for everybody, and that She's A Lady had never been brought to him with all those pretty ribbons and all that wondrous excitement.

And that made him ashamed. Gritting his teeth, he pulled himself as tall as he could, but he still felt woefully small and weak.

Wishing he could somehow alleviate his son's suffering, yet knowing he couldn't, Billy remained on one knee beside him and leaned his head against T.J.'s. The two blond heads—one craggy and marred from years of savage treatment from thousands of punches, the other smooth and unmarked save for the anguished distortion from this latest blow—were together at the level of the waists of the others. The four blue eyes of father and son glistened like quartz stones in a soft, moonlit rain.

It was not often that Billy felt powerless to help T.J., nor was it often that T.J. felt so lost and helpless.

"If she can't run no more," T.J. said softly, trying to control his voice, "I'll take care of her. They don't have to shoot her. I'll do everything. They can just let me take care of her. I'll still brush her and bring her food every day and take her for walks and—"

"Hush now, T.J." Billy hugged him tight. "That ain't right, now. You know how it is with horses. No way to lay 'em down like in a hospital, no way to help 'em heal right. You gotta be a man, now."

T.J.'s chest shook with spasms.

Jeffy turned away from the horse. "I don't understand it," he mumbled. "She was going so good."

"She was out there goin' good," Billy added quickly. "That's right. Wasn't your fault, Jeffy, nobody's fault."

"She was right up there, running so easy. I was just trying to—them two horses got her between—I just—I tried to—do it right—and—" Catching himself before he broke down, he turned away from them all, toward the wall, his clenched hands at his sides.

Billy pulled T.J.'s head against his own, rubbing his hand over his son's wet hair. "Maybe God figures that was her time, when she was happiest. . . ." T.J. shivered in his arm. "A racehorse loves to run, *lives* to run. And if she can't run no more, well, you don't want her to suffer out in some pasture with a bunch of horses she don't like, do you?" He felt T.J.'s quiet sobs under his arm. "You wouldn't want that, would you?"

T.J. shook his head slowly.

"So you want whatever is best for her, right?"

T.J. nodded.

Billy hugged him and closed his eyes. "What a big guy you are, T.J. You are one hell of a man."

T.J. reached up and gently but firmly pushed Billy's arm away. Billy didn't resist. He knew that T.J. had listened, heeded, and wanted to stand tall, just now, on his own.

Billy stood up and backed off a step. He pulled his shoulders back to loosen a cramp from the tight muscles. He happened to glance outside, and he saw her.

Annie Phillips was down the path questioning a stablehand who pointed in the direction of this barn.

Billy stiffened, his face blanched. He hurried outside to intercept her. "What the hell are you doing here?" he said through clenched teeth.

"Is the horse all right?"

Her stylish wide-brimmed hat shaded her face, but Billy could see that her lips were trembling. "Oh sure, the horse is just great! In five minutes they'll probably shoot her. I want to know what the hell you're doing here." He grabbed her arm and pulled her out of sight from the door, around to the corner of the barn.

There she snatched her arm away. "You tried that before," she said, trying to catch her breath. "It didn't work before, it doesn't work now, Billy."

Subdued a little, wishing he hadn't used his strength

on her, he lowered his eyes. "If you hadn'ta come here, I wouldn'ta had to do that."

She rubbed her arm where he had grabbed her, then reached into her purse and took out a cigarette and lighter.

"You want to burn down the barn now?"

"Sorry." She dropped them back in her purse. "I wasn't thinking."

"Big news, you ain't thinking." He studied her face. "So here you are all of a sudden. So what do you want?"

She opened her mouth, then hesitated.

"Come on, after seven years I can hardly wait to hear it."

She avoided his eyes. "T.J.'s Timmy, isn't he?"

Billy slowly shook his head as if bewildered. "You're something. You are really amazing, you know that? You carried him for nine months, right? And now you're asking me if he ain't your own son." He snorted and half-closed his eyes disdainfully. "Even a dumb horse knows its own foal."

She closed her eyes as if he had slapped her. Then she opened them and leaned the slightest bit toward him, clasping and unclasping her hands. "Look, I just want to see him, just to look at him, talk to him for a—"

"After seven years you wanna hold his hand!" He crossed his arms and spread his feet apart, glaring at her. "Let me tell you something, lady. He don't even know you're alive. Know what I told him? I said you were a tramp, no good, that you got killed in a car wreck—" She spun away, but he moved quickly in front of her again. "I told him that the two of us were better off without you!"

Tears welled up in her eyes, and she closed them, turning her head slowly away to one side.

"I even burned all your pictures," he went on, more

harshly than even he had expected, "tore everything out of the scrapbook, burned 'em! You don't exist!"

Her chest heaved a single time, and she opened her eyes. She was more under control now. "Okay, Billy, okay. Look, all I—"

"You're dead, understand! Dead! He's got no mother!"

"Okay, okay." She held up her palms toward him. "Look, Billy, I know how you feel. But I—"

"You don't know crap about how I feel!"

"—But I am his mother. You can't change that. I am his mother."

Her composure frustrated him further, outraged him. "He's got no mother! You're dead!"

She pursed her lips and looked away, as if contemplating. Billy tried to control his panting. At that moment, seeing her there looking so casual, speaking to him with such a calm tone, he could have hit her. Could have broken her fine jaw with either of his potent fists. For a fighter to think that way was frightening, and it scared him. The feeling lasted only a moment.

She sighed and put a hand to her chin. "I just thought I could see him, find out what he's like. Is that so bad? For a mother to want to—"

"Tell ya what he's like," Billy said, wickedly glad for the opportunity. "He's the one-in-a-million kid you dream about, that's what he's like. He's strong and smart and behaves good and don't lie or steal. He's got a heart as big as his whole body, and he's gonna be okay. And you ain't about to see him now or never!"

"Billy, just for an hour?"

She extended a hand and he shoved it away. "No."

Again she pondered for a moment. "You want me to get a lawyer?"

"No." He had answered too quickly. He spat into the dirt.

"Don't drive me to that, Billy. You know as well as I do there's not a court in the country that would deny me the right to see him."

The cords in his neck stood out and pulsed. But he had to control himself, keep from blowing it by words or acts. Her words, her calm suggestion were a threat that stripped him of his confidence. This was tricky ground. He was dealing with a woman he knew well, and who knew him—or used to. He knew her not to be mean or spiteful, but neither was she dumb or weak. She could, in fact, be as tough as anybody he knew. The memory of that sent a chill through him. And here, in this circumstance, she was his equal at least. In a way, he envied her standing there in her silky mint-green dress, her slick heels, her hair done up expensively, surrounding her fine-boned face, and her brilliant wide eyes shielded by that chic hat.

She was a dish, all right, a rich, successful dish. Every inch of her was lean, toned, and tanned. She was a lady. Ladies made him feel crude and nervous. But she had once been *his* lady. And all that wasn't for nothing.

For some moments, as they held each other's eyes, there was an electricity between them, an almost palpable current. A link. They knew each other, all right. And, Billy was sure, she remembered just as he did.

They both opened their mouths to speak at once, when T.J. came bursting out of the barn.

"Champ! Champ! Where are you?" He saw them and ran up. "Doc says no break, Champ!"

"Huh?"

"She's gonna be okay!" Tears were streaming down his face as he slammed into Billy and locked his arms around his waist, burying his face in Billy's side. "No break! She's gonna be okay, Champ! Doc says no break!"

"Okay, okay, take it easy!" Billy grinned, then laughed. He and Annie exchanged unexpected smiles as he stroked T.J.'s head. "So what I tell ya? It all works out for the best!"

"She's gonna heal up good! Nothing serious! Just can't run for a while! Ain't that great, Champ?" He tilted his head back and smiled up, blinking his wet eyes.

"That's wonderful, T.J.," Annie said. "I'm really happy for you—and for the horse."

"Thank you, ma'am." T.J. quickly wiped the tears away with the back of his hand.

"I really *am* relieved. I was very worried. It frightened us all. But now, T.J., what about the other matter?"

T.J. looked at her quizzically, then glanced up at Billy, and looked at her again. Billy eyed her too.

"I bet on your horse," she said with mock seriousness. "You promised me. You owe me ten bucks." She was grasping at anything to keep a conversation going with him.

"I, uh—well, I, uh—sure, if . . ."

She smiled and extended her hand to him. "The name's Annie, remember?"

"Oh, yeah, hi. Sorry about the race. See, it wasn't her fault, and it wasn't Jeffy's either. See, it was just, well, the other horses—"

"Nice to meet you, Annie," Billy put in, pulling T.J. away and giving her a little wave. "And we sure appreciate the invite. Maybe we can stop by sometime. C'mon, T.J., we better get back in there."

He steered T.J. around and they headed back for the barn.

Annie stood for a while as if rooted. Then she took

out a cigarette, lit it, drew a deep breath, and walked
briskly back to her car.

* * *

The Kenyon yacht drew special attention, even among
the other fine boats moored in Miami harbor. Evening promenaders stopped now and then to gaze on
its splendid, sweeping lines, its unmarred white hull
and gleaming teak decks, its spotless ports ablaze from
interior lights, its crewmen at their posts in their
starched whites. The brass twinkled as the yacht
swayed ever so gently from the wake of a passing
sight-seeing boat. Even the mooring lines looked
brand new.

It was a yacht that represented another world, one
unknown to most people, a world of unimaginable
wealth and mobility and luxurious pleasure.

It was a yacht whose owners and guests surely
would have no serious cares in their entire special
world, for surely they would create their world exactly as they wished.

But there were cares within the yacht, and serious
ones. Moreover, these cares would not be unfamiliar
to those walkers who eyed the craft so enviously—had
they known.

"I'm talking about *me!*" Annie said in a strained
voice. "I know what happened, after all!" She stepped
nervously to the porthole window, turned and paced
back, twisting her hands together.

Dolly strode behind her, tapping her cane. "You
think you're alone in this, Annie? How many kids
have been left with aunts, uncles, strangers, or God
knows what?" She stopped to sip from her tall drink.

"This is different."

"Different? Who says?"

"Dolly, it *is*." Annie turned to her and held out her

palms pleadingly. "Don't you *see*? He's right *there*. I could have *touched* him. So *near*, yet, yet—"

"And yet so far, as the old saying goes?"

"Dolly . . ."

"Hmmph." She swirled the wedge of lime in her drink with her index finger. "How many kids spend half their lives without parents? At least he's with his father. And from what I've seen and you've told me, that situation hasn't been a total disaster."

Annie returned to the window. "You're right about that." She smiled wryly. "I guess I *do* sound like a cliché sometimes. Sometimes I think you understand too much. You understand *me* too much. One day I'll probably haul off and slug you for it." She chuckled lightly.

"Hmmph." Dolly slumped into a chair and swirled the ice cubes in her glass. She stared at Annie's back. "You're not so mysterious, you know. You're as selfish as everybody else."

"Well, is it so wrong, so selfish, for a mother to want to see her own son?"

"Nope. I didn't say that." Dolly sighed wearily. "Hand me that bottle of Beefeater's."

Annie turned mechanically to the bar, took a clean glass from the rack, and started to tip the bottle over it.

"*Hand* it to me," Dolly said brusquely, "don't pour."

Annie handed her the bottle.

"And a fresh piece of lime, if you please."

Annie held out the plate of lime slices, from which Dolly took one neatly and dropped it into her glass, following it with a healthy pouring of gin.

Annie watched her. "Look, Dolly, I loved Billy. You know that. It was like he'd just walk in with that silly grin and suddenly the room would seem bigger. I loved him but he couldn't believe it, couldn't be sure. He was so jealous. If I just *talked* to someone—at a party or anywhere—he'd go crazy. He'd want to punch someone out because they'd smile, say hello. He frightened me. A fighter, you know? He never would hit anybody like that, but all that violence inside him. You know what I mean?"

"What I know is that he was a strong, virile, exciting male, a powerful man in his world. And that captivated you. And you were a strong, beautiful, exciting female, who would one day be as powerful in your world as he was in his, and that obviously captivated him. And I suppose some of that still exists in both of you. You both were attracted and frightened by the strength in the other."

Annie stared at her thoughtfully. "I suppose you're right, to a degree. And it was that same odd way, how we got together, the way we met."

"Which was?"

"At a party, no less." Annie paced back and forth, staring off. "You know the kind. Where the hosts try to mix people from the fashion world and the arts with a star or two from the opposite pole. And Billy, he had just become the light heavyweight champion of the world. That fascinated everybody, bored as the rest of us were with talk about our own proper lives. Everybody wanted to talk to him, touch him, touch those hands that knocked people out, touch those muscles, touch that bruised face—you know how it is."

Even as she said it, Annie knew that no one knew how it was. No one had touched him as she had, nor had he touched anyone else as he had touched her. The physical bond between them had been profound. It had not been so at the start, but had become so. She wondered whether the curious paradox she saw in Billy was common to fighters. Fighters made their living in profoundly intimate physical contact—body to body, head to head, trying not only (as opposed to wrestlers) to gain an advantage, but to inflict pain and punishment.

But otherwise Billy did not like to be touched, not gently. He could take a hard punch, not a soft caress. And so in the beginning their lovemaking was raw and fast, with little or no fondling or cuddling before or after.

At first that had disturbed her, for she interpreted it as a lack of real affection on his part. But soon she perceived it more accurately as his fear of tenderness. And as they progressed in learning about each other and becoming closer, it was first he who was willing to touch and fondle and caress. Still he brushed her hands away from him. It was as if he was afraid to let himself go, as if to accept her pleasurable advances would be to weaken himself, make himself too vulnerable.

And indeed, when they finally succeeded together in exploring each other's bodies slowly and at length, it became profound.

She remembered the first time he abandoned himself to her touch. It was on a snowy night in his hotel room in Chicago, with the wind howling off Lake Michigan and the flakes swirling violently around the window. After he had made love to her aggressively three times within an hour, he lay back, drained, exhausted, sweating, and folded his strong arms under his head and closed his eyes.

She whispered to him, "Lie still, don't move, don't talk, let me love you."

And she had made love to him her way for the first time. First she traced the lines of his face with her fingers, then lightly moved down his arms, across his chest, down his legs. She kissed his fingers one at a time, and then his toes. She explored his entire body with her fingers and her tongue. He didn't move, didn't talk, didn't resist.

Finally, after a long time, she leaned on her elbow to look at him. Yes, she had touched him. She had reached him. She had loved him. She leaned slowly over his face and licked his tears away. And then she held him, rocking with him, letting his tears flood over her shoulder.

From then on, sex between them was dramatically satisfying. It was gentle and slow and unmistakably an act of love. It continued to be so, in spite of everything, right to the end, when she left.

Dolly had been pacing during this brief private reverie, and now she chortled. "Yes, I know how it is. I know indeed. It's nothing new. It's a form of slumming—not that I'm knocking that, or him. Men who survive by guts and brawn are always exciting. Lady Chatterley picked for a lover her gardener, after all."

"Billy was more than just brawn," Annie said defensively.

"Of course, of course." Dolly waved her hand. "You don't have to tell me. I'm quite prepared to accept as fact that he had an interesting mind."

"He *did*, and you're teasing me."

"Not really."

"Billy was, well, he was good, and thoughtful, and kind, and—"

"Stop, stop, for Heaven's sake!" Dolly banged her glass down on the table. "Next thing you'll be telling me he would make a great father for your children. You don't have to build him up to me. You loved him, you married him, that's good enough for me. None of that matters now. What I don't understand is why did you leave the baby with him? Why didn't you take Timmy with you when you left?"

"I did." Annie stared out the porthole. "I took him. I took him a dozen times. I'd take the baby and leave, he'd find us. Promises. He'd give me all kinds of promises. He'd make it up to me, it'd all be different. I'd come back, the same thing would happen again."

Annie turned and leaned back against the wall, folding her arms across her chest. "It reached a point—the night of his first fight defending his title, which couldn't have been worse timing—when, I don't know, it seemed like all the doors had finally closed. That was *his* life up there, in the ring. My own was—well, I felt trapped." She hugged herself. "I ran. Picked up and ran like hell. I didn't want him following again, so I left Timmy with him. That was how selfish I was —I left him Timmy."

Dolly arched her eyebrows. "And never looked back?"

Annie blinked away a tear. "Oh, I looked back. I sure did. Phone calls. He'd slam the receiver down in my ear. Wouldn't even talk to me. I sent him letters. Some would be returned to me in another envelope, all ripped up."

"You know he read them. He must have, to go to all that trouble of returning them. And he knew where you were."

"I suppose. Yes, I guess so. But I moved a lot."

"So he also knew you were hurting."

"I guess. That didn't make it any easier."

"I'm sure it didn't. Go on."

"Well, then, after a while, they just disappeared, the two of them. Dropped out of sight. I never dreamed they'd turn up working with horses. I mean, Billy never had any interest, that I knew of." She tilted her head back and closed her eyes. "God, I wanted to be with him. I never knew how much until now."

"Which him?"

"What? Annie's eyes blinked open.

"Which him did you want to be with?"

"Timmy, of course, who else?"

Dolly sighed and shook her head. "Well, that's fate."

"What do you mean?"

"Nothing deep or profound, I can assure you. Just that if that horse hadn't fallen today, you never would have known the child was your son."

"Yes." Annie went to the bar and poured herself a small glass of Scotch. She took a sip and leaned against the bar. "Fate. Although I don't know exactly what it means."

"So what do you do now?"

"Now? Now. I don't know."

"Did you tell him you're his mother?"

"No. I wanted to. I mean I'd like to. I mean, I don't know—I don't know what's best, or . . . damn, what a mess! Dolly?"

"Hmm?"

"I'm glad it happened and sorry it happened, you know what I mean?"

"Yes. But it happened. That's what you have to deal with."

* * *

Billy turned the Cadillac in at the marina and drove slowly along past several yachts until he was near the largest, most impressive of them all. "Wow," he muttered, "must be over a hundred feet long."

"That the one?" T.J. pointed anxiously at the Kenyon yacht while working the index finger of his other hand around under his tight shirt collar.

Billy was wearing his beige check suit, T.J. had on a new white suit, new white shirt, and blue polka dot tie.

"That's her."

"But I still don't understand," T.J. said, slumping back in his seat. "Why do we haveta go?"

"Why you always gotta ask why? What's the big deal? The lady at the track, she thought it would be fun to have us over. People are always inviting other people over to their houses to talk, have some drinks, that kind of stuff."

"You gonna have some drinks?"

"Maybe one or two. Hey"—he smiled at T.J.—"like I told you, them days are over. I'm in training. So don't worry about it."

"People never invite us to parties, not where I gotta wear a tie."

"Well, not for a while, they haven't. But hey, I'm a fighter again. Rich people like to have fighters around. Take some pictures, touch you. Anyway"— he smiled again—"I told them both of us gotta go. Where I go, my kid goes. End of story, case closed."

T.J. pushed out his lips and sat looking at the awesome boat.

"Damn!" Billy slapped the steering wheel.

"What?"

"I forgot to make that phone call. Look, you go on up there." Billy motioned toward the boat. "I'll look for a pay phone. Be back in twenty minutes, half hour at the most. You go ahead."

T.J. put a hand tentatively on the door handle. "What phone call?"

"A phone call, that's all. I gotta tell you about every phone call I make?" He snorted and looked out the windshield. "For chrissake, it's tell me this, tell me that." He leaned across T.J. and flung the door open. "You get out and get on up there. Hold things together until I get back. And watch the mouth. They aren't Beau and Josie, you know."

"What do you mean?" T.J. asked, starting to slide out.

"I mean the language. No swear words, nothing like that. Talk nice, that's all."

T.J. got out reluctantly and looked back at Billy. "You'll be right over in twenty minutes?"

"Or a half hour. Don't worry about it. I'll be there. Didn't I just tell you that?"

T.J. bowed his head and started away. "See you in twenty minutes," he called over his shoulder.

"Hold it." Billy got out and hurried around to T.J. He turned him around by the shoulders and stooped behind him to remove the price tag dangling from his jacket. "That'd look beautiful, you walkin' in there with nineteen ninety-five hanging off your back." He held up the price tag for T.J. to see. "Okay, go ahead on."

T.J. walked slowly away, glancing back a couple of times before walking across the gangplank onto the boat.

Billy turned the car around and drove it out of sight.

Annie watched through the porthole as T.J. trudged across the ramp onto the boat. She saw his brooding face, frowned herself for an instant, then hurried out to meet him.

When he saw her, he quickly smiled. "Hi, Annie. My dad hadda make a phone call, but he'll be right back." He smoothed the sides of his jacket.

For a moment she was puzzled. Then she smiled. "Oh, that's right. Don't you look nice in that suit, though." She stuck out her hand and T.J. took it lightly.

"It's new," he said shyly.

"Well, it's really splendid. But you didn't have to dress up just to come and see me."

"Well, my dad said—"

"I know, and it was nice that you did." She guided him aboard with a hand on his back. "How's your horse feel today?"

"Just fine." T.J. brightened. "She acts like it never happened. Next week maybe we'll start working her, and then Beau says it won't be long until—"

"Mrs. Phillips?" A crewman stepped smartly up and interrupted. "You have a phone call."

"Take a message, please. I'll call back later."

"Pardon me, ma'am, but he said it was an emergency."

"He? Who? Emergency? That just means anything they can't handle at the office. Okay, I'll take it. T.J., I want you to meet Mike, my husband." She called in through the door, "Mike, keep T.J. company for a couple of minutes, will you?" She bent down to T.J. "Tell Mike all about the horse, okay?"

"Sure, okay." T.J. went through the door as she directed, carefully closing it behind him.

Mike sat at a desk, writing. "T.J., just give me a couple of seconds. I'll be right with you. Sit down." He motioned to a chair, then resumed writing.

T.J. sat uncomfortably, folding his hands on his lap and looking around with curiosity, although trying not to be obvious about it, since he hadn't been invited to look around this private, elegant stateroom.

"So, the filly," Mike said without looking up, "she's all right, is she?"

"Yes. Doc said it was a miracle." T.J. leaned forward. "She's not even swelled up." He paused and pursed his lips. He glanced at the door to make sure it was closed. "Can I talk to you honest?" he asked in a lowered voice.

"Sure, what is it?" Mike stopped writing and looked up.

"Well, Annie, she don't understand that when you lose a bet, you lose a bet. I mean, you know, when you bet on a horse, it don't matter what happens to—"

"You mean she wants the money back?" He put his pencil down and leaned back.

T.J. nodded.

"And you want me to talk to her?"

T.J. nodded again.

"Don't you think *you* should do that?"

"Guess you're right." T.J. blushed. "It don't matter." Wanting to change the subject, he looked around quickly. "Who's that?" He pointed at an antique porcelain figurine of a portly old man on Mike's desk.

"This fellow here?" Mike picked it up carefully and turned it in his hands. "This is Thomas Parr. Ever hear of him?"

"No, I don't think so."

"Thomas Parr was an English farmer. He was very famous for having lived a very long time. Can you guess how long?"

T.J. shrugged. "I don't know. A hundred?"

"More than that. Guess again."

T.J.'s eyes widened. "More? Hundred and ten? Hundred and twenty?"

Mike chuckled. "He got *married* at a hundred and twenty. Guess again."

"Wow. Hundred and *thirty*?"

"At a hundred and thirty he was still putting in a full day's work."

"Jeez! Hundred and forty? Fifty?"

"One hundred and fifty-three. The oldest man who ever lived, as far as we know."

"A hundred and *fifty-three*?" T.J. came over to examine the figurine. "Wow, how could anybody live that long?"

"Well, we don't know for sure. And he might have lived who knows how much longer if they hadn't taken him to London to show him to the King."

"Why? What happened there?"

"Actually, he ate and drank himself to death."

"He *did*? How'd he do that?"

"Just put too much food and liquor into a body too old to take it, that's all."

"But how could he get so old? I don't understand that."

"Well, that's my job. I try to figure out why people get old, why some people get old quicker, and some like Thomas Parr live so long."

"Are you a doctor?" T.J. had never had a regular conversation with a doctor before.

"Sort of. I'm a gerontologist."

"A what?" T.J. wrinkled up his nose.

"Gerontologist. A man who studies the aging process. Don't worry, T.J.," he smiled broadly, "I'm not dangerous."

Annie came in briskly, smiling. "The two of you getting along?"

"I was about to tell T.J. about the fountain of youth."

"I could use it. Found another gray hair this morning." She put a hand on T.J.'s shoulder. "That was your father on the telephone. A friend of his is in trouble and he won't be able to make it back until six thirty."

"He can't?" T.J. felt a twinge of panic. "Who's in trouble?"

"Just somebody—nothing really serious. He said for you not to worry about a thing, just make yourself comfortable. And don't make that face. How do you like the boat?"

"Fine." He looked around quickly. "Do you own it?"

"Oh no." She fluttered her hand. "Wish we did. We're only guests here—like you. Know who owns it?"

"Who?"

"You remember the lady with the cane yesterday?"

"You mean"—T.J. assumed a haughty look, pushing out his lips, imitating Dolly—"'Sassy boy, how'd you like your mouth washed out with soap?'"

Annie tried to hide her smile. "Yes, that's her all right."

"Is she here?"

"No, not right now. She's in town. She'll be back

99

later though. You'll like her once you get to know her."

"I didn't mean she wasn't nice or anything," T.J. said quickly, afraid to offend, afraid he might violate his father's trust on language or something.

"Of course not. Come on," she beckoned, "I'll show you around."

They made a quick tour of the ship. The second most interesting thing to T.J. was the lifeboats, slung tight under their davits and covered with bright white canvas. It was not the boats themselves that interested him so much as their purpose. "You mean this ship could *sink?*" he asked incredulously.

"Well, it *could*, any boat *could* sink. But mostly they're there just because it's the law that boats over a certain size must have them."

But most interesting of all was the bridge, with all its technical gear. The captain stood politely off to one side, bowing and answering whenever T.J. had a question. T.J. examined the radar, sonar, radios, compass, intercom, engine controls, peering at each piece of equipment and asking the captain to explain each one.

"Wow," T.J. said, his eyes wide, "it's like being in a *spaceship!*"

Upon leaving the bridge, Annie asked him, "And what would you like to be when you grow up? A boxer?"

"No, I don't think so. My dad says—well, he says it's not so great a life for somebody like me. And it's like, well, unless I could be a champion or something like he is, well, I guess I wouldn't want to do it."

"What then?"

"I don't know. A photographer maybe. You know, take pictures."

"How interesting. Why a photographer?"

They leaned over the rail together and looked off across the harbor.

"I can't tell you," T.J. said softly.

"Why not?"

"I just can't tell you"—he blushed suddenly—
" 'cause you're a lady."

"What? Nonsense. Tell me, come on."

"But you're a *lady*!" T.J. giggled and blushed and
squirmed, crossing his ankles, crossing his arms, not
sure what was bad language and what was not.

"So what? Don't give me that stuff about being a
lady." She punched him lightly on the arm. "I'm
your friend."

T.J. struggled to control himself, gradually quieting
his giggle. "You really want to know?"

"Sure I do."

Words mixing with giggles, he blurted it out. "To
take pictures of naked girls!"

"T.J.!" She tried to keep from laughing, putting a
hand over her mouth. "I'm stunned!"

"See? You see?" He pouted. "I shouldn't have told
you. I haven't even told Josie."

"But why? Why naked girls?"

"Just 'cause. Well, 'cause people like to look at them.
Men mostly. So it would be like, well, I would be
doing something important, 'cause people would like
to look at my pictures."

"I see. I'm not really shocked, by the way." She
patted his head. "I mean, I see nothing wrong with
your wanting to do that."

"I thought you were angry." He looked up at her.

"No, no, just teasing. I'm sorry, I guess I've been
doing that a lot. Who's Josie?"

"A friend of me and the Champ, at the backstretch.
She takes care of me when the Champ's out. I can
really take care of *myself*, but she sort of keeps an
eye on me, and teaches me stuff."

Annie stiffened slightly, taken aback. "Sort of like
a mother?"

"No, just a friend. My mother died."

"Oh . . ." Annie slid her hand down her cheek to her neck, and spoke softly, "She died."

"Yes—but that's okay." He reached out to touch her arm. "It don't matter, Annie. The Champ says she's a beautiful angel who went to Heaven. She's always watching me. At nights she prays for me."

"Oh." Annie blinked several times. "I see."

"And you know what? The Champ says she has blue eyes, just like me."

"He said that?"

"Yup. And like you. You have eyes like that too."

"Yes, I guess so. Probably not as pretty as—your mother's." She looked away, not wanting T.J. to see her face just then, not wanting to look at him. "So—" she cleared her throat, "you like the boat?"

"Yup, I really do. It's nice." He bobbed his head. "It's really nice. Like you see in movies."

"Would you like to go for a swim?"

"A swim?" His eyes widened. "You mean there's a swimming pool on here?"

"No, no, silly." She laughed lightly. "I mean at the beach. There's a nice beach near here. Shall we?"

"Sure! I mean, if it's okay. I mean, if we can do that and still be here when the Champ gets back."

"Plenty of time. Come on, let's go."

* * *

Billy ambled along among the knots of people at the amusement park, some of them leading small fry like dogs on a leash, impatient to move from one game to another, tugging at small hands, remonstrating the children for sticking their thumbs in their mouths. He wondered why amusement parks seemed always to be populated with unamused people. It was not an area he cared much for, and he felt out of place without a child in tow.

But there were other singles like him, most of them

shuffling wearily like sad souls, probably killing time just the way he was. It struck him that none of the others would know why he was there, why he was killing time, just as he had no inkling of why other unattached adults roamed the shabby midway. There certainly are many mysteries in the world, he thought, inasmuch as nobody knows what's really on anybody else's mind; nobody knows what cares and woes might beset such individuals killing time at an amusement park.

Barkers issued their challenges; games plinked and plunked; cotton candy waved in hands like furry wands; unseen sources of music rasped old tunes.

"Step right up," a girl called in a bored monotone, "a real game of skill—no tricks, no gimmicks, six rings for a dollar—toss the rings, win a prize. How about you, mister?"

"Yeah, okay." Billy shrugged. "Gimme six rings."

"Gimme a dollar."

"Yeah, okay." He pulled out a thin wad and peeled off a single. He slapped it down on the counter, and she shoved a pile of rubber rings at him.

"Toss all six rings on the peg," she said, "and win a prize. Step right up," she went on, looking past him for other customers, "toss the rings, win a prize . . ."

She continued to drone her cold invitation while Billy tested the rings for heft. Carefully he tossed them one by one, putting, to his surprise, all of them on the peg. "Hey, I won. Look, lady."

"Hey, pretty good, mister. We ain't had a winner in a long time. Pick a prize from the rack there." She indicated a rack of cheap stuffed toys, then looked at him suspiciously. "You're pretty good. You a hustler?"

"What, for *toys*?" He smiled crookedly. "No, 'fraid not."

"Darn lucky then. Pick a prize. What you want?"

"Gimme that bear on the end, that panda."

"You got it." She picked it down and dropped it on the counter in front of him. "You oughta go again, maybe you'll win another bargain. You're good"—she leaned toward him and winked—"for business—know what I mean?"

"Yeah, I know." Billy noticed some other people edging up, having seen him win.

"How about another six rings then? Win another toy?"

"No thanks." He put the bear under his arm. "I only need one. Good luck."

"You too, mister. Step right up . . ."

He waited until he was back in his car to look at the stuffed bear. When he did, he smiled. Just the thing, he thought, just the right size.

* * *

Annie burst from the waist-deep water, laughing gaily, the sun sparkling off her tanned body and green bikini. T.J. plunged in, then popped up with a mouthful that he squirted at her. Both of them giggling, she grabbed him and hugged him tight for a moment while he thrashed to get away.

At last he wriggled free and dove under again. She plunged in behind him, and when he surfaced, she splashed him from the rear. He spun around, slapped the water with his hand, then flopped in backwards to escape her retaliation.

When he came up, he couldn't find her at first. Then he felt her fingers nibbling at his leg and yelped. He leaped, splashing down on his rear and sinking to the sand bottom. He dared open his eyes under, and saw that hers were open too, looking at him, the water making her eyes dance.

They both stood up, and for a moment her face turned somber as she looked at this eight-year-old boy, so fresh and innocent and happy, at his firm, lithe body already showing signs of fine musculature, at his wet blue eyes; and she tried to imagine the years and years he had already been without her.

But abruptly he dove again, swimming away like a frog, then emerging several yards away, indistinct through her brief saltwater tears. She heard him laugh, then cough. She plodded over to him and pounded his back.

"Swallowed—" he said between hacks, "some water —the wrong way."

At last his coughing stopped. "Wow," he said, grinning, "that was fun!"

They waded together out to the yacht's motorboat, where a crewman sat in the stern waiting to start the outboard engine. He helped them up the ladder. They seated themselves for the ride back, feeling tired and satisfied.

On the yacht, T.J. asked immediately whether the Champ had come, and Mike said he was waiting in the car.

"Well, I better go then, and—"

"First you better change into your clothes," Annie said, waving him inside, "and then we have a few things for you."

"Things?"

"Hurry up and change."

He scampered inside, pulled off his trunks, toweled dry, put on his suit, and stood for a few minutes before the mirror trying to figure out how to tie his tie.

"Hey in there, are you decent?"

"That you, Annie? You mean am I dressed?"

"Are you?"

"Yup, except for one thing." He quickly tried to make an ordinary knot around his neck, and failed.

"Can I come in?"

"Yeah, I guess."

She strode in and, seeing his struggle, laughed. "Forget that. Come on." She steered him out.

Before he knew what was happening, his arms were loaded with gifts—a couple of packages and some fine tack for his horse. He was dumbfounded.

"Don't lose that halter," Dolly said, flicking her cane at the rich brown leather item. "It's expensive."

"Oh, I won't. Gee, thanks a lot." He gazed down at the armload.

"You take care of that filly now." Dolly stepped toward him. "Who's your vet?"

"Doc."

"Doc?" She reared back and laughed. "What in blazes kind of name is that for a *vet?* Pretty high-falutin' if you ask me. I don't know about your Doc. But I've got the best vet in the world. Anything happens to your horse, you call me, understand?"

"Yes, ma'am." He started away toward the gangplank. "Gee, thanks, everybody, thanks a lot. Thanks a million!" Remembering his manners, he came back to shake hands with Mike. "Good-bye, Doctor. Good-bye, Mrs. Kenyon."

He started to leave, then stopped again. He looked back at Annie, who, thinking he had forgotten her, looked stricken. Now she smiled.

"Annie, thanks for everything. This has been one of my most fun days ever. And, and"—he looked down shyly, then back up at her—"and you can come and see me, at the backstretch, anytime, if you want."

She knelt happily in front of him and took his elbows in her hands. She wanted to hug him, hold him, keep him there. But she just smiled and said, "I will, I will come and visit. I had fun too. Good-bye."

He nodded, waved, and hurried off the boat. Once on shore, he waved back, then disappeared into the parking lot.

Annie stood staring after him, lost in thought.

"My dear," Dolly said, "you do have a problem, I believe."

"What?"

"I said, you have a problem. Get ready to suffer."

Annie, as if suddenly awakening, blinked several times, then looked at Dolly, regarding her with melancholy trust. Dolly, for all her harsh airs, was eminently perceptive and kind. Yet her words caused Annie sadness for that very reason: The grand woman was probably right; Annie would probably suffer more over this new circumstance in her life.

Somehow Annie felt that she had no right to love her son so. So little did she know of him that he could be any little boy, but for the fact that she knew the truth. He could be just any nice, fun, well-behaved little boy, but for the fact that, as Billy so savagely reminded her, she had carried him in her womb for nine months. How much did she want him really? Did she want a child with her as she traveled the world, worked night and day in the fashion business? Was it perhaps just guilt that so impelled her into re-acquaintance with Timmy—T.J., as he was now known?

Her feeling of loss when T.J. left the boat was doubled by her feeling of resentment toward Billy—resentment because of the very fact that Billy had clearly done a good job with him, that those two were so obviously close and harmonic. For all the pleasure she felt at having given T.J. one of his "most fun days ever," she felt locked out.

Annie turned from Dolly and went inside to Mike's study.

Mike relaxed in a lounge chair reading. "Go well with T.J., did it?" He smiled warmly to her.

"Yes." She was so glad she had Mike to talk to—Mike, so steady and calm and understanding. "It really was a nice time." She sat down on the sofa opposite him. "Today in the water I could actually feel his heartbeat." She stared off, a slight smile on her lips. "This beautiful child, and I thought, He's mine, he came from me." She lowered her eyes. "Congratulations. Congratulations to me for nothing." She looked wistfully at Mike. "He is what he is, and I had absolutely nothing to do with it."

"Come now, I don't think you had so little to do with it, Annie. You were there the first year, which is so important."

"You know what? Suddenly, out there, I wanted to bundle him up and hop aboard a plane bound for somewhere far away."

"I wonder how Billy would feel about that," Mike said evenly.

"Mmm." Annie mused. "I'd be taking away the only thing he's got." She was silent for a time. Mike did not return to his reading, but watched her patiently.

She was pensive. "Coming back in the outboard I could feel T.J.'s eyes on me. Very serious. Finally he said, 'You've got pretty skin, Annie.' Just like that. I laughed, made a little joke, and he said, 'You got any kids, Annie?' And all of a sudden I was just jabbering—'Look at that sky, T.J.! How deep do you think the water is here? Aren't those trees over there on the shore lovely, T.J.?' He probably thought I was crazy, but I couldn't look at that face and say, 'No, I don't have any children.'"

She stood up, Mike stood too, and she leaned into his arms. "Darn it, he's growing," she said, nuzzling his shoulder, "he's changing. I want to see that. Am I crazy? Am I totally wrong?" She looked up at him, resting her chin on his chest.

"No," he said softly, hugging her, "that's not wrong."

"It must seem very strange for you, all this. After

so long, to suddenly have T.J. and Billy brought into your life."

"Not really. They have always been a part of your life, and you are such a big part of mine."

"Oh, Mike." She held him tight. "I don't know what to do."

"Sometimes you don't have to do anything," he said, caressing her hair. "Sometimes you just have to let things work themselves out."

She closed her eyes and wondered how anything like this could ever work itself out.

* * *

T.J. hustled through the parking lot toward Billy's car, happily toting his presents. Billy was slumped behind the wheel, his old leather cap tipped down over his eyes.

"Hey, Champ?" Billy didn't move. T.J. dumped the gifts into the seat and climbed in beside him. "Hey, Champ?"

Billy gave a start and opened his eyes. "Jeez," he said, yawning and stretching, "I musta conked out there. So"—he rubbed his eyes and looked at the pile of things—"you had a great time, right? They gave you a lotta food, presents, made a big deal outta you, right?"

"Uh-huh," T.J. said brightly. "Presents for *us*, Champ! Look." He held it up. "Got a halter musta cost fifty bucks! And look at this—two lead lines, brushes, curry comb . . ."

Billy picked up the halter and looked at it. "Rather have a rope halter. Works just as well, and you don't have to clean it. But this is nice." He tossed it into the back seat.

"They were nice people, Champ," T.J. went on, his eyes glowing with pleasure. "They were rich but they were really nice. Not like most turf-clubbers with their noses in the air." He tipped his nose up in snooty fashion. "Annie was really nice. And you know what?"

"What?"

"Her husband is a jerrytologist."

"Jerry who?"

"Well, a doctor. The old lady—" he wrinkled up his nose thoughtfully. "Rich but nice. Dolly, her name is. And Champ, we went *swimming!*"

"You did?" Billy started the car.

"Yup. Me and Annie. She's really a nice lady. You would really like her if you got to know her."

"Really?"

"Yup. And then we . . ."

As T.J. prattled on about the boat and the people and the gifts, Billy reached into the back seat and surreptitiously tossed out the cheap stuffed bear.

CHAPTER 5

Billy had learned to gamble as early as he had learned
to fight. His parents were migrant farm workers, and
his earliest recollections were of picking apples and
peaches and cherries in Michigan and living in a little
shack near the orchards. He bet other kids he could
pick more, then fought to protect his winnings.

Back then, fighting and gambling were part of the
same matter, and totally under his control. He could
outwork and outfight anybody—no luck was involved.
Billy always had strength and tenacity; his father
taught him how to use his dukes. Other kids tried
to get you in wrestling holds, trip you up, but his
father taught him how to jab with his left to keep
them back, double-jab with his left and follow with
his right when they straightened up, hook with his
left when they went for his waist to wrestle him. He
was quick; his father taught him footwork. So he could
dance and he could punch. Other kids who learned
the game developed good right hands, but Billy had
a left as well. Because it was such an advantage,
he developed that left hook to a fine art; it was today
his best punch.

But gambling, as he grew up, became a different
matter. When he wasn't making it with his fists, he
was trying to make it against the odds. Trouble was,
gambling was no longer a matter of outworking and
outhustling anybody, it was a matter of luck.

Luck, to somebody like Billy who had never relied on it, was not kind to him. It was as if luck, having been disdained by such a self-reliant person as Billy Flynn, was taking its revenge. For the once he won so big, big enough to buy a horse, he lost a thousand times. But for that once, Billy was hooked forever. He ignored the truths of the odds, always figuring his time was near, his success just around the corner, his pot there for the taking on another roll of the dice. And he went at it with a fervor that suggested victory would be his on his intensity and will alone.

So now he rolled the dice again, and again the stickman droned, "Seven—a winner."

Billy grinned across the table as more money was raked in to add to the sizeable piles that already flanked him.

Other players mumbled and groaned, onlookers gasped.

"Oh, we got our hot shooter here, folks," the stickman said. "Everyone get down, he's comin' out."

Billy shook the dice, cupped them, blew on them, closed his eyes. "Full odds on the eight and here's another hundred on the hard way!" He flung them out.

"And the point is eight!" the stickman barked.

Cheers and applause arose from the onlookers; other players shook their heads.

Billy grabbed the dice and shook them again. "Whuddya need when ya walk down Broadway?" he sang. "Well, here's—uh—wait a minute." He tossed the dice to the stickman. "Gotta take a leak, Whitey. Sit on 'em for me. Back in a sec."

Billy walked quickly out of the gambling room into the small lobby and banged through the flimsy door of the men's room.

A few seconds later, through the front door walked Mike Phillips. He stood letting his eyes adjust to the dim light, then saw the crowded crap table in the next room. He was about to head in when Billy emerged and brushed past him. "Billy Flynn?"

Billy stopped short, turned slowly, and regarded Mike with suspicion. "Who wants to know?" He sized Mike up quickly. "You a cop, mister?"

"I'm Mike Phillips."

Billy stared at him, then abruptly turned away and started toward the table. "We shoot the bull some other time, mister. Right now I got a hot pair of dice with my name on 'em."

"I have to talk to you," Mike said, reaching to touch his arm. "You got just one minute?"

Billy stopped and looked down at Mike's hand with hard eyes. Mike dropped his hand. "Not now, buster, I'm a winner."

"I'm Annie's husband."

Billy eyed him for a few seconds. "Outside."

In the parking lot, Billy leaned back against a car, arms folded across his chest, glaring at Mike. "So here's your minute. Talk."

"We've got a little problem." Mike's tone was serious but not unpleasant.

"I ain't got a problem. I got rid of that problem. I got rid of that problem several years back. You got a problem maybe."

"I want to talk about the boy, Billy."

"You do? That a fact?" Billy started pacing back and forth. "What'd she do? Cry a little, get you to come down here? She feel like a mother now?"

"Yes."

"It's too late." He wheeled to face Mike. "And you! You better be careful. Who the hell're you to come messin' in my life?"

"I'm married to the mother of your son. Maybe you don't like it, but that's the way it is."

"Yeah, that's the way it is all right." Billy took a

step toward him. "That's right. And you're damn straight I don't like it! T.J.'s a beautiful kid. He's healthy, happy, and he's gonna stay that way! Where she is all the time, I don't know. But the track's the greatest place in the world for a kid to grow up!"

"I agree with you, Billy."

"Oh, you agree with me, huh?" Billy was confused for a moment. "You do, huh?"

"It's a beautiful place for a kid to grow up. A kind of paradise. And when I saw T.J., I said, My God, what a wonderful child. My hat's off to Billy for the job he's done."

"Oh yeah?" Billy spat into the dirt. His head pounded, and he almost reached for his aspirin.

"You've been a wonderful father."

He was unsettled by this man, this husband of his own former wife, this calm, direct man who seemed unafraid even though Billy could break him into small pieces if he felt like it. "He knows his manners," Billy said gruffly. He turned toward the door. "I gotta go. I'm on a hot streak."

"You can't walk away from it, Billy. He has a mother."

He wheeled back. "He's got no mother!"

Mike took a tentative step toward him. "He's the one who decides that. It can't be you, Billy."

"I gotta go." His temples throbbed.

"What happens ten years from now when he finds out he had a mother who wanted to be with him? How will T.J. feel toward you then?"

"Yeah, well, the future ain't my bag. I worry about that when the time comes."

"*His* future? Isn't that your bag?"

"I gotta go." Billy strode to the door. He put his hand on the knob, hesitated, then spun back. "Mother! Some goddamned mother!" The words boiled out of him. "Never does nothin' for him! Now after seven years it's 'Oh my, oh my, I just love that boy so much, I just never knew it!'" Rage and sadness clenched his throat like a fist, and he almost choked. He jabbed at Mike with his finger. "Never does she change his pants, wipe his nose, teach him his prayers, give him a bath, teach him right from wrong—but what difference does that make?"

The pain in his head making him dizzy, he swung the door open and went inside, slamming it behind him.

Reality, for Billy, was taking and giving a punch, working hard for a day's pay, seeing T.J.'s eyes light up when something good happened. None of that pertained to the roll of the dice. Not in his eyes. The reality of the dice was something he could not really see. For the reality was that the odds would beat you, every time, in the end. Had Billy been able to face that, he wouldn't be in the situation with which the long night finally presented him.

All the other players had finally left; dealers stacked and counted the night's take.

Billy leaned over the table on his elbows, head buried in his hands. It had all turned bad after the meeting with Mike. That had soured things, disturbed his concentration, caused the dice to roll short. He had, of course, stuck with it, watched his pile dwindle, felt the harsh grip of the loser seize his neck, and known how it would end. Known but refused to know. He could feel it turn. But for Billy the gambler, the errant hope was for the game to be infinite. In time he would go back up. But the game was not, is never, anything but finite. It always ends when there is nothing left. It ended for Billy when there was less than nothing. And he had made his tragic offer.

Whitey the stickman paced back and forth near him, shaking his head. "A horse," Whitey rasped in his gravel voice. "What am I gonna do with a damned horse?"

"The horse cost six grand," Billy mumbled, closing his eyes against the pain in his head.

"Billy," Whitey put a hand on his shoulder, "we go back a long time. Bring me the two thousand inside of forty-eight hours and the horse stays where it is."

Billy looked up at the man, looked at his wiry body, his slicked-back hair, his dull brown eyes, his thin lips. "I bought it for my kid," he said in a voice almost a whine. "It's gonna break his heart."

Whitey held out a pen and a piece of paper. "Here, sign an IOU for the two grand. Forty-eight hours you got." He patted Billy's shoulder. "Last thing I want to do is break a kid's heart. I got a kid of my own."

Billy signed it gratefully, seeing Whitey then as the kindest of men, his benefactor. A man needed his friends. And he had learned his lesson: He would not gamble again. Or else he would quit when he was ahead.

T.J. was sleeping when he got home, a couple of hours before dawn. He tiptoed over and looked down at him. T.J.'s blond hair, damp with perspiration, clung to the side of his face. His small arms circled the pillow. One leg was cocked, the other straight, as if he were about to jump over something. His breathing was even.

Billy dared not touch him, even though he wanted more than anything at that moment to pick him up, hug him, tell him everything was okay. Or maybe what he wanted was for T.J. to tell *him* everything was okay. If he really was a good father, here was the evidence. T.J. was strong, a good kid. Without T.J. he was nothing. Not any more. Not until he climbed into the ring again. And even then, it would be to show T.J. what he really did for a living, what he did to really count for something. And he needed to do that to deserve T.J. All else was sham. A son needs to see his father work—he believed strongly in that.

Of course, there were other reasons for going back to the ring. So many that it was too complicated to think about—money, fame, challenge, ego, even vengeance, all the rest. He needed to do it to reassure himself that he was not growing old, that he could still use his dukes, that the former truths still existed for him, that he was Billy Flynn, champion of the world, now and forevermore.

And that T.J. would be deservedly his, now and forevermore.

He found himself strangely wishing that T.J. would never grow up, never grow older, that he would always be T.J., this size, this age, this dependent, this trusting. He knew he wouldn't—Billy was not blind to certain biological truths—but there was still time, at least, for Billy to shape up and show T.J. what his father could do—which was what he did better than any other man his weight in the entire world.

He longed to pick him up and tell him this, about how good he was in the ring and how good he would be again. But he dared not disturb T.J.'s peaceful dreams. And so he quietly went to bed to grab a couple hours' sleep before hitting the telephones to collect old debts.

T.J.'s dreams were not all that peaceful. He dreamed of huge ships sailing on vast seas, and of people dressed in suits and ties. And nobody would listen to him as he went from ship to ship in a lifeboat begging them to stop and wait for the Champ, who was out there in the water somewhere. They said it didn't matter, it didn't matter, he would be there when they got back, he would be there when they got back.

But T.J. knew it wasn't true, knew they were never going back. They didn't even know him, the Champ.

They just said they did. They didn't know who he was talking about. They were just being nice. Rich but nice. And they hugged him and gave him presents, but they didn't understand that the most important thing was the Champ, swimming out there somewhere in the warm, deep sea. And they were never going back because they would sink. . . .

He awoke with a start and sat up. He was breathing heavily, and sweat ran down his face. It was hot in the room, but not that hot. He remembered the dream and shivered. He looked over at the Champ, sleeping quietly. He wanted to go to him and talk to him and make him feel better.

But the Champ needed his sleep. That would help him get in shape. Then he could run four miles and do push-ups and sit-ups and punch the bag and spar in the ring with those other fighters who weren't nearly as good but would help him get his timing back.

There wasn't much T.J. could do to help him get in shape, but at least he could let him sleep. He tiptoed over to the window and looked out. He couldn't see anything but dark fog. That made him uneasy—fog was like a dream—and he quickly slid back into bed.

He didn't want to go back to sleep right away, not until the dream was safely gone for sure. He reflected on his day on the boat. People like Annie and her husband and Dolly, they were nice, but they didn't know the Champ. They could never understand how good the Champ was, how important. Doctors and people married to doctors and friends of doctors could never understand what it was like to have a fighter for a father. And he could never say to that doctor, Annie's husband, that he looked so soft and skinny in that suit compared to the Champ, who had such big muscles and moved smooth like a cat. He wished the Champ had been there on board the boat so they could see how strong he was.

And he was sorry that the Champ hadn't been there, because it was so hard to explain to him how nice everybody was. T.J. even felt a little guilty about having such a good time while the Champ had to deal with a problem.

Suddenly he felt *very* guilty because he realized that in his happiness in showing off the gifts, he had never even asked who it was that was in trouble, that the Champ had to telephone about.

But everything was okay now. The Champ was there sleeping. It would be morning soon, and they would be out together working the horses. As long as the Champ was there, everything was okay. Happy and secure, he fell asleep.

Before T.J. awoke in the morning, Billy was up and gone. Finding the gym still locked, he was on the phone in a decrepit booth outside. His feet crunched on the broken glass from the doors, his eyes scanned idly the obscenities and invitations scrawled on the box. A hand over one ear to shut out the sound of early morning buses, he was making the latest in a series of similar calls.

"Sure I understand, but how about this?" He thought for a moment. "You give me three hundred and I wipe the slate clean. How's that, huh? Deal? . . . Hey, I don't care what time it is." His voice grew harsh. "It may be early for you, but it's late for me . . . Hey, it's Billy Flynn talkin' here, you fat welcher!"

The phone went dead in his hand and he held the receiver out in front of him and glowered at it. He clenched his hands, controlled himself, took out his address book to find another number, and dialed it.

"Hello, Marty there? . . . He is? Good. Tell him Billy Flynn is callin'." He waited. "What? Whaddya mean, he ain't there? You said he *was* . . . Well, you tell him he owes me and he better come across, got that? . . . Yeah, tell him that. And tell him I'll stuff it up his nose if he don't!"

He slammed the receiver down and banged out through the door, and stood on the sidewalk panting with anger.

So that was how it was when you came to collect from all those leeches. Billy ground his teeth together. So that was how it was when you weren't the Champ any more. Well, he would get it all right. He would get it, and he would get back. He would remember. Billy Flynn wasn't about to forget who was with him and who wasn't. What goes around, comes around. And he would be around, one fine day.

He got into his car and squealed away from the curb. He wanted to get back to the backstretch and say good morning to T.J.

T.J. was playing a hose over She's A Lady when Billy arrived. "Hi, Champ," he called.

"Morning, T.J.," Billy said, walking up and tousling his hair. "How's she goin' this morning?"

"Fine, Champ. See?" He pointed to her leg. "No swelling at all. She's puttin' weight on it and everything."

"Good, that's real good. Sorry I wasn't here when you woke up. Had some errands."

"That's okay, Champ. I had breakfast with Josie. I can take care of myself." His chest pumped up with pride.

"That you can, T.J., that you can." He patted the flank of She's A Lady. "She'll be running soon."

"Yeah! Doc says it won't be long."

"Well, we don't want to rush her. Got to give her time. Got to remember how lucky it is she's still around at all, after what we thought."

"Yeah, I do. Luck was with us, right, Champ?"

Billy studied his glowing eyes. "Yeah." On impulse he suddenly grabbed T.J. and swept him up in his arms, the hose spraying down his back. He hugged him and swung him around. "We got her on our side, all right! Long as you and me got ourselves, we also got old Lady Luck!"

"Right, Champ! Hey, you're gettin' all wet!"

He put him down. "Don't matter. Feels good. Okay, I got to get to work."

Billy went to work mucking out stalls, carting the old stuff off to the pile in the wheelbarrow, laying down fresh beds of straw. Toward noon he was pushing a wheelbarrow full of dirty straw and manure away from the stalls when he saw She's A Lady walk into the area, Beau leading her and T.J. on her back.

They came up to him, and Billy patted the filly's damp neck.

"Want to ride her?" T.J. asked.

"No thanks, not just now. Got a couple calls to make, soon's I dump this load. You get your chores done?"

"Yup, every one."

"Good. See you in a bit."

Billy went into Barn Eleven, where there was a pay phone on the wall in a hallway. He checked his book, then dialed. "Harold? It's Billy, Billy Flynn . . . Right. Look, I need your help. That thousand I . . . Hey, don't give me that crap. I've seen you at the track—the clothes, the broads—you're flush! You got plenty! . . . Look, you little weasel, I carried you when—"

The phone went dead. Only the fact that there were other workers in the barn kept him from tearing the phone off the wall. Through the door he could see T.J. brushing his horse with great devotion and care. The sight bothered him under the circumstances, made his flesh crawl with anger and frustration.

He gritted his teeth. "Somebody gotta come across," he muttered, heading for his car.

He stopped at two addresses, finding neither of the men he was looking for, before stopping at the coffee shop. He placed another call on the wall phone, nodded, hung up, and came over to sit at the counter.

"What'll you have?" asked the waitress, wiping the counter in front of him.

"Coffee." He pinched his eyes. "You got any aspirin?" She shook her head.

"Alka-Seltzer maybe?"

"We don't have nothing like that. Sorry. Cream and sugar?"

"Black."

"Place across the street, a drugstore, they'd have it."

"Gotta wait for a call, somebody's calling me back."

"Headache?" She put the cup in front of him.

"Yeah. Thanks." He held the cup in both hands and stared at it, watching the steam curl up. He sipped his coffee slowly. The call didn't come. He had figured it wouldn't. He tried to stem the tide of panic creeping into him. He ordered another cup and sipped that. No call, nothing he could do about it.

He needed something to take his mind off the phone and his head. Swiveling on his stool, he saw a newspaper strewn on the seat of a booth. He went over and picked it up and sat down in the booth to scan it.

He wasn't interested in big news or long stories. He leafed through the pages looking at the fillers. A small item caught his eye. He sat up straight, gaping.

"Holy bejesus," he muttered to himself. "So she's doin' big-time fashion shows now, huh?" He thumped his fist lightly on the table. "So that's why she's down here." He thought for a while, staring at nothing. "Worth a try."

It was hard to sleep that night. He and T.J. had talked for a while, mostly about She's A Lady and the scuttlebutt around the backstretch. Then they had hugged each other, T.J. had kissed him on the cheek and gone to bed.

But Billy lay awake, playing and replaying over in his mind what he had to do and how he would go about it, complete with dialogue. It was well rehearsed by morning, but Billy knew it wouldn't happen that way. It was like fights; set them up as carefully as possible in your mind, they never came off quite that way in the ring. Somebody had a punch you hadn't figured, a move you hadn't counted on, a strategy you didn't expect. And it was good that you could work outside of the script to adjust. That's why he relied upon his own strengths and skills rather than an opponent's weakness. He could handle whatever they threw and find the openings for himself. In the ring you couldn't hide anything, and nobody was better than Billy Flynn at thinking on his feet.

Except for that once, that last fight, when he wasn't relying on anything at all, or looking for anything. Ironic how that time related to this. This would be, however, somewhat different from the boxing dialogue in the ring, and he was not confident by mid-morning when, dressed in his suit, he headed his Cadillac out of the backstretch.

He wheeled into the courtyard of the magnificent Viscaya Museum, an impressive, massive stone structure that had once been a personal estate. It had cost millions when it was built at the turn of the century, and on this day it was attended again by pomp and style and opulence. The courtyard lot was filled with luxury cars—Mercedes and Cadillac limousines and Rolls-Royces and Jaguars.

Billy found a spot into which he could wedge his old Caddy and walked uncomfortably past the liveried chauffeurs who lazed by their limos. Such wealth and class made him uneasy.

He did not see the reaction of a group of three chauffeurs, nor did he hear their comments after he passed.

"Hey, you know who that guy is?"

"For sure he ain't rich."

"He looks familiar, sort of."

"That's Billy Flynn."

"Who's that?"

"Billy Flynn, dumbo, he was once light heavyweight champion of the world."

"That a fact? Fight game sure takes it outta your hide, don't it?"

"Yeah, he sure looks beat, all right."

Billy went in the grand front entrance, where a uniformed guard stood watch. Billy went up to him. "Fashion show?"

Without speaking, the guard nodded the direction.

The marble entry hall, with its frescoed ceilings, heavy statuary, and huge plants draped from giant urns muted the sounds coming from the end of it, the direction Billy had been sent by the guard. But the sounds he heard were unmistakably Annie's amplified voice. First he could see the TV crews with all their equipment and lights, and the flashing bulbs of the still photographers, and the correspondents with their notepads.

And then all around them he saw the lavish displays of fashion set up in various specially erected rooms for the purpose: a boudoir for lingerie, a tack room for riding outfits, a ballroom for gowns, a disco for the display of current styles. Some of the clothes were new, some old, representing historic fashions; some clothing was on plastic models, some on flesh-and-blood ones that didn't look much different to Billy.

Up above, on a balcony, a combo played music of various styles and periods.

Now he saw her, on an elevated stage in the middle of everything. Her glasses were perched on the end of her nose, and an elegant bag hung from her shoulder. In one hand she held a microphone, with the other she pointed out certain features of a colonial gown on a model standing beside her. All around her were the press and the beautiful people of the fashion world.

Annie was, Billy thought—resisting an urgent impulse to flee—impressively all business, and he had absolutely no business being here amid such a fine crowd. But now he was indeed in the midst of it, and he didn't even dare to turn around. And so he watched her and listened. He *beheld* her, so awesome was her command of this company.

". . . Diana Vreeland's marvelous exhibits at the Metropolitan Museum in New York, the costume exhibits at Los Angeles Art Museum, and"—she waved her arm grandly, looking up, and in so doing sighting Billy, which caused her to falter slightly—"and, uh, and this splendid exhibit here at Viscaya . . ."

Billy held her eyes for an instant, grateful for her slight lapse, which gave substance to his intrusion. In the same instant he was so struck by her, seeing her in such a context for the first time since their divorce, pained by the awareness of her beauty and strength and the audience she held rapt by her poise and words and by the fact that this elegant and commanding lady had once been his.

". . . bear glowing testimony to that assertion." She cleared her throat and looked over his head.

"I'm confident that it will not be long now before universities confer honorary degrees on fashion designers and . . . "

The high-flown words clamped his head in a vise, the room danced before his eyes. He could not stand being so out of place. It had been a mistake. He abruptly turned and pushed back out through the crowd.

She saw him leaving. "And now," she said hurriedly, "for an appreciation of this beautiful gown created by the great Charles Frederick Worth of Paris"—she gestured toward the model—"I'll now turn you over to Bruce Glass, who knows more about this period than anyone else."

"I do?" Bruce was startled when she handed him the mike.

"You better," she whispered back, quickly stepping down from the stage. She scurried out and through the front door, stopping on the steps to look hastily around. Then she spotted him heading away through the lot, shoulders hunched, hands jammed in jacket pockets. "Billy! Wait!"

He stopped and looked around, and she waved and trotted up to him. "Billy! What is it? Is everything all right?"

He frowned at her as she tried to catch her breath. She looked unnerved, and he liked that. He liked to see her uncomfortable, since he had been so uncomfortable inside—and coming here in the first place, for that matter.

"Is everything okay?" she repeated, reaching out toward him.

"It was stupid," he growled, "me comin' here. I don't know why . . ." He looked past her at the Museum. "I see you up there, all those people . . . It was stupid." He shook his head. "Just stupid, that's all."

The irony flashed through her that his feeling must be akin to the one she had when she watched him fight. "But what's the problem?" She searched his face and saw only anger. "Is it Timmy? Is he all right?"

"T.J.'s fine," he said, emphasizing the initials.

"Then what?"

He wanted her to squirm for a while, because he would shortly have to squirm in telling her.

"Please tell me why you came."

"I gotta have a reason to go everywhere?"

She shook her head slightly and looked into his eyes.

He knew she wouldn't ask again. So he said, in as firm and straightforward a tone as he could muster, "I need a favor."

She questioned with her eyes.

"Those guys"—he looked off to the side, curling his lips defiantly—"all those guys, the years I was on top, all the money, they forget me now."

Still she questioned him with her brilliant eyes, parting her lips a bit but not speaking.

"But I'm not here to beg," he said with a wave of his hand, "I want you to know that."

She nodded silently.

"I just thought, hell, maybe once, just once I ask."

"Please ask, Billy."

"Then I say, no, she won't do it."

Slowly regaining her composure, she took a breath and fingered the silver necklace at her throat. "At least tell me what it is before you decide that I won't do it." Unlike him, she did not like to see her former mate stand here so discomfited.

Looking off, he mumbled something she couldn't hear. Then he looked at her and said briskly, "Two thousand dollars. I need two thousand dollars."

"Okay."

"What?"

"I said okay. It's all right."

"You don't even know what—"

"I don't need to know anything." She took her checkbook out of her shoulder bag and unclipped the pen from it and began to write.

"It's no big thing," he said, staring at the checkbook and hoping his face wasn't red, "I want you to understand that."

"I understand."

"Don't make any difference if you give me the money or not, I still feel the same about everything, what you done, how it all—"

"Shut up, Billy," she said calmly, "just shut up." She tore out the check, blew on it to dry the ink, and handed it to him.

He took it without looking at it and stuffed it into his pocket. "I want you to understand this is just business," he said gruffly. "Ain't that what you're all about—just business?"

She didn't answer, nor did she look away. He was sorry he had said that. He softened his voice. "Don't know when I'll be able to pay you back." He looked at the ground.

"Whenever. It doesn't matter. I'm glad you're doing this."

"Doing what?" She was smiling at him, which made him nervous. "What're you talking about?"

"The money." She arched her eyebrows. "For him, I assume, for Timmy."

"You know about that, huh?"

"I don't know about anything, Billy, except that I can't imagine you coming here for anything less than Timmy—certainly not for yourself."

"I lost his horse gambling, that's why I came here. I need two grand to get it back before T.J. finds out."

"Gambling." She put a hand to her lips. "I'm sorry."

He felt that she truly was. "Yeah, some things never change, right?" He turned and started away.

20

"Well, see ya around." Then he stopped. "You know what? You looked good up there."

"Thank you."

"Couldn't figure out what the hell you were talkin' about but you sure looked good sayin' it. Big shot now, huh?"

She shook her head and held up her hand, then walked over to him. They walked slowly together through the parking lot.

"You want to know the truth, Billy? There are no big shots. Not really. Just big circumstances."

"You always did have a head on your shoulders." He chuckled. "One of the things about you I went for."

"Until I wanted to use it."

"Huh?" He stopped to look at her.

"You wanted me to be smart, Billy, but you didn't want me to have a life of my own. I'm not blaming you, it's just a fact."

He resumed walking with her. "Well, times change, people change. In those days, I wanted a wife to be around when I needed her—in the house, waiting for me. Bein' the Champ and all that pressure, training, keeping sharp, getting exhausted and punched out and all that. I needed somebody to—to—"

"To soothe your fevered brow? To bring you your pipe and slippers? To give you a rubdown? To shake her head over your new bruises and bumps?"

He blushed at the accuracy of her words. "Just to be there," he said softly.

"Billy, even that wasn't enough finally. You resented my attention. You resented being dependent on anybody for anything. You didn't want me to leave and you didn't want me to stay. But mostly you didn't want me to have any part of my own life separate from you."

"Well, today I feel absolutely the same."

"Attaboy, Billy." She tapped his arm with her delicate fist. "Hang in there."

"Only kidding."

"But not much."

They had reached his car and he turned to her. "Not much." He patted the fender. "Remember this baby? After the Perez fight we go into that showroom. I say, 'That one,' and whammo, we drive out with it. Six grand I pay, all cash. Remember?"

"I remember."

"Yeah, just what I paid for that horse. Six grand. And plenty more where that come from, in those days." He studied her, pursing his lips. "Can I ask you a question."

"Sure."

He thought for a moment. "All these years it's been there, this question. Like a little rock inside I can't get rid of." He put a hand on his stomach and squeezed. "Just sittin' there in my gut, this question."

"What?"

"The fight." He looked off. "I'm in my corner and I look around and you're gone. The seat's empty. You were there, then you just disappeared. Why'd you do that?"

Her mouth dropped open. "You ask *me* why I did *that*? *Why* I did that? What did you expect?"

He shrugged his shoulders, looking like somebody feeling the cold.

"Okay, okay," she waved her hand, "let's drop it. It isn't anything to talk about. I don't want to argue."

"You can't just tell me why, nice and simple."

"Not if you don't know why already. It never *was* nice and simple."

Abruptly Billy pulled the car door open and slid into the seat. "Makes sense. No big deal then, no big deal now. See ya around." He turned the key but the engine didn't catch.

She leaned in the window. "Billy, I appreciate what you said. What you told T.J. about his mother."

He tried the ignition again. "What're you talkin' about?"

The car started. She sighed and stepped back. "Good-bye, Billy."

*　*　*

A new group of horses was due to arrive at the Kenyon stables in a different section of the backstretch sometime that evening, and T.J. wanted to stay up to see them. He hadn't associated Dolly with those stables—hadn't even seen her before that time at She's A Lady's race—until they talked about it on her yacht. But now he was interested, and he knew they would be fine horses.

He and Billy sat on a rail near the barns and chewed sticks of hay.

"Think they're comin', Champ?" He crossed his feet just like Billy.

"I don't know no more than you do—less, probably, since you talked to the old lady."

"I hope they do. But I also hope they're not better than She's A Lady."

"Only know that when she runs against 'em on the track."

"Hope she can run soon." T.J. leaned against Billy and yawned.

"Give her time. Tired?"

"Little. But I don't wanna go up. I like sittin' here with you."

"I like it too. Just don't pass out on me and fall on your head."

"I won't." T.J. laughed.

But in time he did—he fell asleep, not on his head. Billy cradled him in his arms and carried him upstairs and laid him carefully on the bed and started pulling off his clothes.

T.J. woke, blinking. He pushed Billy's hands away and sat up, rubbing his eyes. "I can take care of myself, Champ." He started pulling off his own pants.

"I know. Just didn't want to wake you."

"The horses come?"

"Nope, you didn't miss nothin'."

"Good."

T.J. finished undressing and lay back down. Billy leaned over him, mussed his hair, pecked him on the cheek. "Get a good sleep, see you in the morning."

"Aren't you coming to bed, Champ?"

"Soon. Just gonna sit downstairs a while, then I'll be up."

"Good. See you in the morning." T.J. closed his eyes.

Billy sat on the bottom step looking out into the night. Beau came by.

"Saw you sittin'," the old black man said. "Somethin' the matter?"

"No, nope. Just thinking."

"You thinking 'bout the ring?"

"Oh, maybe."

"Heard you were comin' back."

"Yeah."

"Well, I *heard* you were gonna make a comeback, but I don't *see* you doin' it."

"Pretty soon, Beau, pretty soon I'll start getting in shape."

"Why you comin' back, Billy?"

"Oh, I dunno, prove something, maybe."

"Folks don't care all that much for somebody provin' somethin' again he already proved once. And you proved it once, what you could do."

"Prove it to myself then, maybe. Prove I can still do it."

"Well, I sure hope you can. All of us here, we your friends. We want you to make it, whatever you do."

"I know. Appreciate it."

"And your boy. T.J. wants you to make it too."

"Yeah."

"But he don't know, does he?"

"Huh?" Billy looked up at the wrinkled brown face.

"He don't know about fightin', what it really means."

Billy squinted at him. "What are you tryin' to say, Beau?"

"I'm sayin' you know, and I know too. I used to fight once. Just a kid. But I know. I know like you do. 'Cept I never had none a the good parts. No championship, no big arenas, none a that. But I know." The old man's watery eyes were narrowed, and he gave Billy a queer look he didn't understand. "It's awful hard, Billy, awful hard." He turned and started slowly away. "Be sure, Billy, just be sure."

Billy didn't understand that either. He watched Beau walk under the streetlight that lit the backstretch and fade into the night. He had never known old Beau had been a fighter. Never would have guessed it. But then, how do you know about an old man, unless he tells you?

Billy rose, stretched, and headed upstairs to see if he could get some sleep for a change.

CHAPTER 6

Billy slept late. T.J. hustled downstairs to take care of some of his early chores for him, wanting the Champ to get good and rested.

In another area of the backstretch, a trainer for Dolly Kenyon's stable led a mare around in slow circles before her owner.

Dolly cast a critical look on the horse, appraising her with expert eyes. "She looks thin, Ralph," she said, tapping her cane, "tired."

"Yes, ma'am." The trainer nodded. "I reckon so."

"She's had it." Dolly started walking away. "Ship her north. Time to breed her."

"Yes, ma'am."

She walked by Barn Eleven, where a goat trotted over to nuzzle her for a handout. "Shoo, you." She waved her cane menacingly. The goat backed off, but followed at a discreet distance—the goat, like many people familiar with her ways, knew that her "no" might soon become "yes," soft heart that she really was.

Dolly came upon T.J., finished with his chores and now grooming She's A Lady, who was tethered beneath the portico of the barn.

"You brush her any more and she'll go bald, T.J."

"Hi, Dolly! She likes it. Really." He continued brushing.

"I'm sure she does."

"I brush her twice a day."

"Hmm." She looked over the horse with narrowed eyes as T.J. brushed. "Bad to love 'em too much."

"Why? How can you love a horse too much?" He stopped and looked at her.

"Because they can break your heart. They're very fragile, very beautiful. Magnificent. Like dancers, boxers. A couple of seasons they can race, then it's over. They can't run as fast, compete as well, and no one cares. These beautiful, beautiful animals." She ran a hand down the smooth neck of She's A Lady.

"I'll always care." T.J. resumed his brushing. "No matter what happens, I'll keep her and care for her. I don't care if she can race or not."

"Hmm. The best go out to pasture to breed. The others may wind up in a dog food can." She shook her head. "Strange business. Very sad sometimes."

Billy had come down at last, and T.J saw him.

"Hey, Champ! Hey, Champ, come here! Somebody you should meet!"

Just then a white Cadillac pulling a horse trailer turned in and came to a stop behind Billy. He turned to see it. "Hang on, T.J., in a minute."

From the Cadillac stepped Whitey, the stickman from the gambling house. Flashily dressed in a red check blazer, white pants, and a white snap-brimmed hat, he leaned back against the car and folded his arms.

"So?" Billy walked up to him. "So what's this. What's the matter? You don't trust me? I told you on the phone last night I'd bring the two grand this afternoon."

"So I recall," Whitey said, his eyelids drooping lazily.

"And what's the trailer for?" Billy hooked a thumb at it.

"For carrying a horse, that's what for. You think I drag around a horse trailer for the hell of it?"

"For carrying what horse?" Billy cocked his head warily.

"Hey, Billy," Whitey spread his arms, "you know what horse."

"Now hold on," Billy spread his hands out in front of him and stepped back, "just wait a sec. What the hell is this? We had a deal. Last night you're happy I got the dough."

"Always happy when somebody's got some bread, chum. But the deal was forty-eight hours. The deadline was up ten hours ago."

Billy's fingers dug into his palms. "What the hell you tryin' to say, Whitey?" He beckoned with his fingers. "Come on, say it."

"Look," Whitey sighed and folded his arms, "I gotta draw you a picture? I changed my mind. I sorta like the idea of owning a racehorse."

"Yeah," Billy's lips curled meanly, "come on. So what?"

"So I'm taking your horse over there."

Billy exploded. He lunged into Whitey, slamming him against the car with a metallic thump that could be heard far down the backstretch. Then he fired a series of quick, short punches with both hands as Whitey started to slide down the door.

"Champ, don't!" T.J dropped his brush and came running as he screamed, "Don't, Champ!"

"Christ, he'll kill him!" shouted Josie right behind T.J.

"Security!" somebody yelled. "Call security!"

Billy finished Whitey off with a right to the belly and a left uppercut, then stood over his crumpled form with fists ready for more. "Get up, you bastard! Get the hell up!"

Three security guards raced onto the scene. The first reached for Billy, and Billy wheeled and chopped him down with a right at the base of the jaw. Hands bleeding, he mashed a right into the mouth of the second one, who dropped to the ground, then he dispatched the third guard with a left to the Adam's apple, leaving the man gagging and stumbling backwards.

"Champ! Champ! Don't!" T.J. was at his heels, reaching for him.

Dolly grabbed T.J. from behind and pulled him back.

"Stop, Billy!" Josie hollered, not daring to get in his way. "Billy, for God's sake stop! Billy!"

Billy stomped wildly around, his crimson hands set to deal with anybody in his way. Whitey started to move, and Billy headed back for him, when the siren blared.

The police car, red light turning and siren howling, skidded to a stop at his side, and two officers sprang out and dove for Billy, each pinning one of his arms.

Billy struggled ferociously for a minute, then the strength seemed to flow out of him. He seemed suddenly drained of everything, and he slumped in the arms of the two officers.

"Champ!" T.J. wailed, still held in Dolly's arms. "Champ!"

The officers pulled Billy's arms behind him and snapped on the cuffs, then led him, head down, feet shuffling, to the squad car. They pushed him into the rear seat, one got in beside him, and they sped off.

"Champ!" T.J. sank back against Dolly, tears washing down his face, and he reached out a hand as if he could pull Billy back. "I want to go with you, Champ!" Then the stength flowed from him too, and he collapsed in sobs as the police car slid around the corner of the backstretch and was gone.

"It's all right, T.J.," Dolly said softly, hugging him. "Don't worry, he'll be fine. He just lost his head for a minute. He'll be all right. We'll all help him."

"Champ," he moaned weakly. She held him as his crying softened. His eyes were closed, but this was worse than any dream.

*　*　*

Attorney Robert Adelman, a bulky, square-faced bear of a man with beetle eyebrows, showed no emotion in his face, as usual. While this was not a routine case for him, it had certain routine elements. He sat at the table in the visitors' room at the jail, his fat briefcase on the floor beside him, his hands folded on the table in front of him, his unblinking eyes following Billy as he paced the room.

"The judge who will be handling the hearing is a friend of mine," Adelman said in a low, matter-of-fact tone. "As far as the newspapers are concerned, the police report of the incident will be mislaid temporarily. The only real problem as I see it is the broken jaw suffered by one of the security guards, and it is my understanding that Mrs.—"

"An animal!" Billy hissed, staring at his fists. "The poor guy's only trying to do his job and I brain him. Like a damn animal . . . " At that moment Billy wished he could turn his fists on himself, so filled was he with revulsion at his action—stupid and misguided actions for anybody, inexcusable for a fighter.

"I've talked with this Whitey fellow," Adelman went on calmly, as if he were explaining the terms of a lease. "In view of the fact that he is operating outside the state gambling laws, he doesn't wish to discuss this with a judge. He's decided not to press charges."

"Thank him for me," Billy said bitterly.

"I could have you out of here very quickly, Mr. Flynn. Perhaps tonight."

"Tell 'em to forget it. Don't matter when I get out."

He frowned at his battered knuckles. He faced the wall. "Why the hell are they doing this, whoever hired you?"

"My clients' motives are not my concern, Mr. Flynn." Adelman hesitated, cleared his throat, then proceeded. "Beyond the more immediate task of getting you released from jail, Dr. Phillips has discussed . . ." Billy whirled and fixed him with an icy glare, and Adelman's words trailed off. Looking at the table to avoid the hostile look, Adelman went on. "Mrs. Phillips is, um, concerned about her son." He looked up. "I'm sure you can understand that."

"Champ!" T.J. was at the door. "Hi, Champ!"

"I know how hard this must be for you, Mr. Flynn."

"You don't know nothin'," Billy snarled, avoiding T.J.'s wide eyes. "Just shut up. And get outta here."

Adelman nodded, picked up his briefcase, and slipped out of the room.

T.J. rushed in. "Hey, Champ, how ya doin', Champ?"

Billy looked at him, but neither smiled nor spoke.

T.J. held up a small brown paper bag. "I figured you was hungry, Champ, so I brought you some barbecued spare ribs."

"I'm not hungry."

"Okay, Champ." T.J. put the bag on the table, trying not to show his disappointment. "It's okay. Anything you want, you just let me know, Champ."

"And from now on," Billy turned away, "you stop callin' me Champ. Champion don't use his fists outta the ring."

"But, but—" T.J. took a couple of steps toward him. "but he wanted to take the horse! You were right!"

"Horse don't make no difference!"

"But She's A Lady, she's my—"

"I had no right!" He clenched his hands and stared at the wall. "I'm a bum!"

T.J. had never seen his father this way, and it

frightened him a little. He didn't want to say the wrong thing. He wanted to cheer him up. Most of all he wanted to be close to him. "When they gonna let you out? Did they say when you could come home?"

"Don't know yet. A month, could be six. Who the hell cares?" Billy knew who cared, and he knew who he himself cared for more than anybody or anything else in the whole world. But he felt that he had defiled his love for T.J., made himself unworthy of this trusting boy's love. He wanted more than anything to hold him, talk to him, make things right. But he couldn't, and so he wished that T.J. had not come. "Look, there's something you and me gotta talk about."

"Sure, Champ. Oh!" He clamped a hand over his mouth, then dropped it. "But I *can* call you Champ, can't I really?"

Billy ignored the question and guided T.J. to a corner where he squatted down to face him at eye level. "Listen, T.J. You know that lady from the boat, the one you're always goin' on about how nice she is?"

"Annie?" T.J.'s eyes brightened immediately; he was relieved that they could turn to a more pleasant subject.

"Yeah, Annie. Well, I want you to do me a favor."

"Anything, Champ! Anything!"

"Go stay with her for a while."

T.J.'s mouth dropped open. He blinked at his father. "Why?" he asked softly. "Why can't I stay at the track? I can stay with Josie. She's right outside waitin' for me, and—"

"'Cause I say so and I'm your father and that's the end of that!" Billy rose and turned away. T.J.'s pure, innocent presence was pushing him to the edge.

T.J.'s voice came even softer. "Why are you sending me away, Champ?"

For a moment Billy's shoulders rose and fell with

his breathing. Then he turned on T.J., erupting: "Because you're a regular pain in the butt, that's why! Can't go anywhere without you naggin' at me—Champ do this, Champ do that! Go to have a drink, you're there sayin', 'No, Champ, don't!' Go to play some cards, I got you tuggin' at my belt! I'm *sick* of you tuggin' at me! *Sick* of feedin' you! *Sick* of takin' care of you! *I'm sick of you hangin' around!*" He spun back toward the wall, his chest heaving.

"Please, Champ," T.J. pleaded in a small, strained voice, "anything you want is okay." He gulped. "I won't hang around you if—if you don't—if you don't want me to."

"You're goin'!"

"Please, Champ . . ."

"No! No more! You're goin'!"

T.J. choked back tears. "Champ, I'll do whatever you say when I'm with you. I'll be somebody when I grow up. Somebody like you. But I won't bother you, I promise. Please, Champ . . ."

"Shut up!" Billy took him by the shoulders and shook him. "I don't want no more back talk! I want you to go!"

"No!" Suddenly the tears burst from T.J. "No! It ain't true! You don't want me to go! You're a liar!"

Billy slapped him. They were hushed, staring into each other's eyes like statues frozen in the moment of truth.

Then T.J., still holding Billy's eyes, took a slow step backward. "Okay, Champ," he said quietly.

Billy worked his lips, but couldn't speak. He closed his eyes.

Josie, hearing the commotion, came to the door and stepped quickly in to pull T.J. to her. She glanced at Billy, then down at T.J. She tried to turn him away to go out of the room, but T.J. resisted being turned.

He backed slowly out, never taking his eyes off Billy's face.

But Billy never opened his eyes to see. He could not open his eyes until the sounds of their footfalls faded away down the corridor. And even then he couldn't open them for a while. Tears oozed out from beneath his closed lids. Then slowly he opened his eyes to look at his hands.

"I hit my own kid," he mumbled. "My own kid. I hit T.J." He smashed his fist into the concrete wall and held it there against the cool stone, watching a trickle of blood roll down, marking the gray wall like a network of veins.

Then he slumped to his knees and bowed his head. But he offered no prayer. He felt unworthy even of asking forgiveness. He stayed in that position as if awaiting the executioner's sword.

❊ ❊ ❊

T.J.'s eyes were dry. He felt numb. Josie didn't try to make conversation. In silence they drove to the marina, and she walked with him to the boat. He carried a small, soft, lumpy suitcase. She stood with him at the gangplank, holding his hand, both of them looking straight ahead at the splendid yacht.

Then, pressing his hand, she said, "T.J., we all love you. And we love Billy too."

T.J. nodded.

"And She's A Lady, we'll take care of her."

T.J. nodded again and, feeling the unfathomable sadness well up in him anew, quickly dropped her hand and hurried onto the yacht.

Josie had called ahead, and Annie was waiting for him, alone on the deck as Josie had suggested.

T.J. avoided Annie's eyes as he came aboard. He stood silent before her, head down, as if awaiting punishment.

She touched his cheek lightly with her fingers, then took his hand to lead him to his room.

A party was going on in the main salon. Luminaries of the fashion world, several designers, models, mingled with racehorse owners and other old friends of Dolly. The guests were, as usual, enjoying Dolly's gruff hospitality.

"Drink up, drink up," she urged as she circulated, "don't be shy." A waiter maneuvered among the guests, offering a tray of canapés.

"As for me," Dolly told a knot of fashion people, "this cranky old lady will stick with what she's got. I can't afford to keep up to date with your fancy dresses *and* keep my horses."

They laughed, delighted with her irreverence. They all knew that Dolly's wardrobe cost as much as anybody's.

Annie came in and went directly to Dolly. "Excuse me," she said, turning Dolly away from the guests. "Dolly," she said confidentially, "I have to skip your party. I don't want to be rude, but it's T.J. I really didn't expect him tonight. But he's here, and with all these strangers it might be hard on him. I think I should be with him. Am I forgiven?"

"Forgiven?" Dolly huffed. "Rot! Has he eaten? He must be starved. You get in there to him with some food, Annie! He's more important than all these freeloaders here, and don't you forget it."

Annie smiled and started away.

Dolly stopped her. "What's the story on Billy?"

"The lawyer's working on it."

"Well he *better* be, that old bimbo, at his prices. Keep me posted."

"I will. And Dolly? Thanks."

"Beat it."

T.J. opened his suitcase with dreary resignation and stood staring at the hastily packed contents. He didn't know what was in it. He didn't care what was in it. He didn't care about anything except the Champ. He tried not to think about the Champ, because he didn't want to cry. And he dared not look around the room, because it was so strange and fine and fancy. It made him feel small and homeless and alone.

But he couldn't force the Champ from his mind. The slap was nothing—didn't even hurt. But the words, they kept echoing in his head. Was it possible that he had been in the way all these years? That the Champ had simply tolerated him, and not loved him like he said so often?

Well, he loved the Champ. That would never change. And when the Champ got out of jail, he would help him any way he could—help him train and get in shape. And if the Champ didn't want him around, he wouldn't be around. He would find other ways. He would help the Champ any way he could his entire life. He would always love the Champ. It didn't matter what the Champ did or said. Nobody was as good and strong and—

"T.J.?" Annie opened the door quietly and leaned in. "I brought you some food," she said brightly, coming in with a tray and closing the door behind her. "You must be hungry."

He tried to smile, but his lips quivered. "Thanks, but I'm not hungry, Annie, honest."

"Well, just in case." She put the tray of sandwiches and milk on a table and sat down on the small sofa behind it.

T.J. took his toothbrush and tube of toothpaste from the suitcase and walked into the bathroom to put them on the sink. Noises from the party reached the cabin.

"T.J., I guess you can hear the party. I know all those people would seem strange to you. So I thought

145

maybe I could just stay in here with you for a while, okay?"

"Okay, Annie," he said, coming back to the room. "But I like parties. We have parties all the time on the backstretch." He started lifting things out of his suitcase and piling them up beside it. "Doc, Josie, Beau, Jeffy—the Champ." He hesitated. "The Champ —likes beer at parties."

"I know." Annie saw his shoulders tense at the mention of the name, and wanted to change the subject. "Tomorrow morning we fly to New York."

"New York? You do?"

"Mike and myself, and you, okay? It's where we live. Ever been to New York, T.J.?"

He turned to her. "The Champ and I went to Atlanta, Georgia, once. He had a meeting with some people. About fights, you know? I waited in our room, so's I wouldn't be in the . . . way."

"New York is very big. I'll take you to the top of some of the tallest buildings in the world. On the weekends we'll go to the Bronx Zoo or ice skating in Central Park. Can you ice skate?"

"No."

"Don't worry, we'll teach you."

"Thank you." T.J. felt a lump in his throat. So much was happening at once. He was overwhelmed. He didn't care about New York, but he was glad Annie was here. "You're a very nice lady, Annie."

"Well, thank *you.*"

He resumed unpacking. He took a dirty shoebox with a string around it from his bag. "Where should I put this, Annie?"

"On the desk for now." She watched him do it. "You must be tired."

"A little, I guess."

"I know this must have been a very hard day for you."

146

"Well, it's harder for the Champ. He's in—" He couldn't say the word. He felt the lump in his throat again and fought it back.

"I'll help you off with your clothes."

"No thanks, Annie. The Champ says the day a man can't take off his own pants he ain't a man."

Annie chuckled. "All right, sit on the edge of the bed, I'll help you off with your shoes."

"I can take off my shoes. Honest, Annie."

"Come on," she knelt in front of him and reached for a foot, "let your mother do it." She started to unlace a shoe when she sensed his look. She looked up at his face. His eyes were quizzical. "You mean," she said so softly as to be barely heard, "the Champ hasn't told you yet?"

"Told me what?"

Without thinking, she blurted, "T.J., I'm your mother."

T.J. narrowed his eyes. "You're not my mother."

"But I am." She tried to smile.

"My mother's dead." His voice had a hard edge.

Now it was out, and she had to convince him quickly, otherwise it was, to him, a blasphemy. "T.J.? Listen to me, please." She put her hands on his knees and looked into his unbelieving eyes. "Your mother isn't an angel up in heaven. Because I'm your mother. I'm right here and I love you."

His look was stern and cold.

"I love you very much, T.J."

T.J. squirmed away from her. "What're you talking about? You can't be my mother."

"But I am, T.J. I am your mother." Such a neat statement of fact, such a firm and consoling truth; yet she was desperate, in fear of losing him totally for her enunciation of it.

T.J. crossed his arms. His voice came firmer now,

strong. "You don't live with us. You're not married to the Champ. How can you be my mother?"

How to assail this simple logic, flawed as it was? "Please, please, T.J. Just listen, listen closely to me for a minute. Let me explain. You see, you don't have to live with someone to love—to be—"

"You love the Champ?" His eyes challenged her.

She couldn't answer.

"You don't love the Champ! *I* love the Champ, not *you*! You don't even *know* him!"

"Please . . ."

T.J. pushed her away and lunged for the far corner of the bed, where he sat crouched like a cornered animal. Tears dripped onto the bed. "You're not my mother! You're not! My mother's dead! And she *is* in Heaven like the Champ said! He don't lie to me! Don't you come close to me! I don't want you! You're not my mother! I don't need no mother! I got the Champ!"

Annie straightened up and took a stumbling step backward, her hand over her mouth. His hateful look cut her like a knife. She couldn't hear more. She fled the room.

Once coming to the free air of the deck, Annie breathed deeply, then walked forward to the bow—to be as far away as she could from the happy babble of the party. She looked out over the harbor. Moonlight flickered on the corrugated crests of the silken black water. Lights on other boats beamed like eyes and seemed to be staring at her. She clasped her arms around herself and shivered. The pain was deep within her; and, as if to free it, she opened her mouth in a silent, tearful scream.

* * *

Jail didn't matter; Billy was not anxious to be free. The sounds didn't disturb him—the clanking of the heavy steel doors, the raucous laughter of the cops or guards somewhere, the soft blues chant of another prisoner nearby; he couldn't sleep anyway.

All he had done as a father to give T.J. the best shot at a decent life for himself—better than his own—seemed wasted. Worse than wasted, destroyed. Wanting only to protect T.J., he had himself inflicted the wounds. Just a dumb punk used-up fighter was all he was. Violent, nasty, dangerous even to his own kid.

His only hope was to get back in the ring and prove to himself and everybody else that he was not gone. That his fists were not relegated to cheap, back-alley brawls, but were the fists of the Champ and still the Champ. Maybe all that ferocious anger that exploded on him back on the backstretch was just because he had no outlet for what he had trained most of his life to do.

Maybe. But that didn't explain why he had slapped T.J. If asked to explain it, to say the first thing that came into his mind, he would say, "because I love him." That didn't make any sense, yet it was the purest, most certain of truths.

Just as it was a pure, certain truth that he had loved his own father. His own father had left him, just as his own mother had left them both some months before that. Life had been so hard for those two, he understood that now. His parents had to work so hard in the orchards just to survive that they hadn't had much left for him, for each other, for anything.

They lived in that one-room shack—it seemed to be the same one-room shack wherever they were picking. There never was much conversation. Just eat and sleep and pick fruit. Fatback bacon and beans they picked themselves. Apples and pears, of course, but that was taking money out of your own pocket. Milk when a farmer let them near a cow.

At the time, it didn't seem like a hard life to Billy, because he didn't know any other kind. His friends—those boys he met at the beginning of each picking season and lost at the end, seldom the same ones from year to year—lived the same way. Billy learned to depend on no one, to take care of himself, to steel himself against hardship or loss. He survived with his sweat and established himself with his fists, just as his father had done.

His father was tall and lean and strong, and he coughed a lot. Why he coughed was never discussed; there was nothing anybody could do about it, whatever it was. People lived as long as they lived, that's all, which was as long as they could work.

When his mother left, his father never discussed that either. One summer, instead of working in the orchards, his mother had been hired to work in the farmer's house. The farmer was an old, wrinkled, hard-bitten man who never talked. His wife was dead. So Billy's mother worked in the house. And the farmer had a son. The son was handsome and lively and pleasant and liked to come out to the orchards and talk to the workers. Apparently, one day he just moved out of his father's farmhouse, taking Billy's mother with him.

As he lay on the bunk in jail, Billy tried to remember his mother. She was blond, like his father, but beyond that Billy couldn't really conjure her up. He didn't know if she was good-looking or not. He could remember next to nothing about her.

She left when he was twelve. His father never said anything about it, but he seemed to weaken after that. He still went out into the orchards every morning, but he couldn't bring in as many bushels, and he seemed to be more stooped and tired.

And then one morning he was gone. Just gone.

Billy woke up to find the shack empty. Nobody had seen him go, nobody knew anything.

So Billy was on his own. He continued working in the fields and fighting to keep what he got. By fifteen he was a fighter, a real one. A man from the Police Athletic League got him bouts. He got him into the fight game as an amateur, and soon Billy got himself into the fight business as a pro.

There were a lot of losses in the beginning, when Billy met guys who really knew how to fight, while he was just learning the art inside the ring, within the rules. But later on Billy stopped losing. Other people became interested in him—promoters, trainers, hustlers. Soon the P.A.L. was forgotten, Michigan long gone. He was in Chicago. He had a manager who cared for him, protected him, steered him right. His name was getting in the papers.

By the age of twenty-three, he was ranked among the middleweight contenders. By twenty-five he was bigger, a light heavyweight. By twenty-seven he was a contender. By twenty-nine he was champion. By thirty he was retired.

All those years, as he thought about them now, seemed telescoped into a much shorter span, like a week. All the hard work and pain and sacrifice were forgotten. It all seemed unreal.

But it was real. As real as the fact that by thirty-seven he was here, in jail. He wasn't champion any more. He wasn't married any more. His son was gone.

Even his love was real. That was the hardest part. Billy loved hard. In those early years as a fighter, there wasn't much time for it. Oh, a few chicks and broads here and there. But no love. Everything was invested in fighting. He was always what was known as a "hungry" fighter—that kind with a special craving for the win, the kind that will do anything to beat you, which includes years of almost savage, unyielding dedication to tuning your body and skills and a willingness to absorb the lonely, unforgiving pain and punishment that each fight brings. In the ring, Billy Flynn was the hungriest fighter alive.

But that didn't come cheap. When he became champion, he allowed himself to fall in love for the first time. He fell in love with Annie. And he fell hard. He was consumed with it. He wanted her to be everything to him. She was his new hunger. He wanted her to fulfill all the needs of love and fidelity and home that he was so hungry for. But that heart so strong for the ring was not capable of adaptation to anything less than total victory. Annie could not be everything to him, and so she would be nothing. And so she was gone. In the middle of that fight, she suddenly was gone. And that same heart was riven. With Annie gone, it no longer served him in the ring. And nothing meant anything to him any more.

Except T.J. Again Billy loved hard. And now T.J. was gone. If not really gone, at least sent away. Maybe because Billy was afraid he would lose him anyway, one way or another.

The familiar vise clamped his head, searing his temples, as he lay on the cot in jail. He put his fists over his eyes. It didn't help. He wouldn't ask for aspirin. He wouldn't ask for anything. He richly deserved every discomfort. He wished it were worse, even as the pain forced a moan from his lips.

The next day he was led before the judge. He stood there beside the lawyer and heard the judge accept his guilty plea on some ridiculously diminished charge and solemnly sentence him to a few weeks in jail, sentence suspended. He was free.

That's what the lawyer said, he was free. He did not feel free. Spared, maybe, but not free. He was still trapped by what he had done. He hurried from the courtroom, not even thanking the dour lawyer. He wanted to get back home, to the backstretch.

* * *

In another part of the city, in a dingy room behind a door with a frosted glass panel on which was painted in old-fashioned gold lettering GOODMAN SPORTING PROMOTIONS, INC., Charlie Goodman huddled with two other men in shiny suits and open shirt collars. The three sweated in the airless chamber.

"So who?" one of the men asked.

"How about that new kid, Rubin Gorewitz?" the other asked, scribbling the name on a pad.

"He don't call himself that no more," said the first.

"What then?"

"Goro. Rubin Goro."

"Okay, how about him, Goro?"

"Nope," Goodman said. "He's already on the way down."

"Fisher then, Davey Fisher. Got a good—"

"Forget it," Goodman said. "Black wouldn't draw flies."

The three sat thinking, each doodling on his pad.

"Fast Eddie Pollitz?" the first man suggested hopefully. "At least he's white."

"That's also the *most* he is. Look." Goodman slapped his pencil down. "We gotta fill an arena with this fight. All you guys keep comin' up with is no-count bums."

"But Charlie, don't you wanna ease him in? Get him started with a breather, somebody he can—"

"He's thirty-seven, for crissake! We ain't got time for breathers. This has to be a big fight. Gotta be somebody with a whole lot to gain by gettin' into the ring with him."

"You mean somebody on the way up, that could take him?"

"Right."

Goodman wrote a name on his pad, circled it, shoved it out on the desk in front of him. "That's it. That's him."

The two men looked at the name.

"Bowers?" said the first man, looking at Goodman dubiously.

Goodman nodded.

"But Jesus, he's a *tank*, Charlie. He can take a head off with his right hand."

"Yeah!" said the other man.

"That's right. Hell of a fighter. Looking for a title shot himself. We beat him, we might get a title shot ourselves right away."

"And if Bowers *does* take his head off?"

"That's why we gotta fill the house. Roland Bowers, that's the answer. Former Champion Billy Flynn versus top contender Roland Bowers."

"Man, that fight would really pack 'em in, that's for sure."

"Right. And that means, whichever of them wins, we win. Okay, get your tails moving. Let's set it up."

* * *

Billy sat on the lower steps leading to his room, between Beau and Josie, enjoying the cool night breeze.

"Lucky about that suspended sentence, Billy," Beau said. "Who was that lawyer?"

"Appleman, something like that."

"Yeah, well, that's a name to remember. Must be a legal genius, pull that off."

"Connections. That's all it is, connections. Just like the fight game." He spat into the dirt. "Makes you wanna puke sometimes."

"Still good you got off, way I see it. You shouldn't oughta be so glum."

"Sorry."

"Yeah, get your chin up. Just think, crowd's on its feet, you're climbing through the ropes. You the Champ, remember."

"Yeah. Some champ."

Beau yawned, stood up, and stretched. "Well, think I'll get some shut-eye. You oughta get some too, Billy. You got a long road to go, lotta work to do. We're all behind you, you know, all us here. But you gotta do the work."

"Yeah, you're right." Billy chuckled. "Right as always. Good night, Beau. And thanks."

Beau waved and walked off toward his room.

A horse whinnied from a stall nearby and was answered by another. Josie studied Billy, who was staring at his boots.

"Feeling pretty down, huh?" She put a hand on his arm.

"Yeah, guess so."

"Missing T.J.?"

"Yeah, guess so."

They were quiet for a while. Then Josie said softly, "I've got a fifth of brandy up in my room, Billy. Want to crack it? You'll be able to sleep."

"No, not tonight." He sighed. "I'd be no good. I'd fall out of the saddle. But thanks, Josie."

Josie laughed and rose to go. "Good night, Billy."

"Night. And Josie? I ever tell you you're one sexy woman?"

She waved him off, laughed, and went on.

Sometimes Billy liked to sit alone like this, alone with his thoughts, enjoying the cool night air. But not now. He felt alone enough already. What he wanted most to do was sleep, to shut out his loneliness. He went up the stairs to bed.

THE CHAMP

* * *

It was already hot and humid at four thirty in the morning when Billy twisted to the side of the bed and sat up. Dawn was just hinted on the horizon. He slumped over and tried to shake the sleep from his head.

He was going to run four miles this morning. He had to start getting in shape. Even though a bout hadn't yet been fixed, he had to start. It had been such a long time.

He traced his hands along his legs—still lean and firm. He traced his fingers over his chest and belly—not so lean, not so firm. He didn't like the small rolls over the band of his shorts. Not a pot, but not so hard as it should be. He ran his right hand up his left arm, then his left hand up his right—the power was still there. Strength in the arms was the last to go. And he worked hard with his arms in the backstretch.

He dragged himself erect; then, putting his hands at the sides of his waist, he rotated his upper body back, to the sides, forward. The back was tight. So much needed for the legs came from the lower back. If the lower back failed you, the legs were gone too. He needed knee bends, sit-ups, push-ups, stretches, all the rest. Many kinds of exercises would be in his repertoire for getting in shape. It would be a little while before he started hitting the bag. Then sparring, that would come last.

First came the roadwork. Four miles. A lot to start with, after so many years, but none of it would be easy. It never had been, and Billy never shirked.

He pulled on his trousers and a T-shirt and heavy army boots—the last to give his legs even more work. Then he sat again on the edge of the bed. The feeling was completely familiar: He didn't want to do it. But, sighing, he headed out.

The first half-mile, around the barns and onto the service road, was a killer. Before his lungs and heart really kicked in, he was running on will. He pushed through that, got a wicked mile behind him, then headed back.

Four miles was beyond him this first time out; two would do. By the time he got back to the base of the steps to his room, he was drenched in sweat, the shirt and trousers stuck to his body, the boots weighed a ton, his head weighed two tons. His back hurt, the pulse pounded in the sides of his neck and beat his temples like a hammer.

But he had begun. From this day on he would work. There would be no stopping him. Because he knew that right now, this very day, out of shape as he was, he could knock somebody out with either hand. He was not in championship shape, but neither was he flabby. By fight time he would be able to dance, jab, and hook a full ten rounds if necessary. He was hungry.

He felt a brief elation at this self-assessment, and that was enough to carry him up the steps and into his room, where after stripping his soggy clothes and dousing himself in a quick shower he collapsed on the bed.

The day was as hot and humid as had been promised at dawn, and Billy wearily hotwalked horses, mucked out stalls, moved bales of hay and straw around, cleaned tack, and did whatever jobs were required. By late afternoon, the work was done and so was Billy, nearly.

He brought out She's A Lady and brushed her down, combed and curried her as conscientiously as T.J. would have done had he been here. Josie had offered to do it, so had Beau, but Billy insisted on taking care of her himself. She was sleek and frisky, a fine horse for the money—maybe even better than that, with how she looked in her first race before going down.

Billy found himself wondering about Whitey. He hadn't gone back to the gambling parlor, and doubted that he would. And he was sure Whitey wouldn't come around here again. Billy had sent him the money, and that should be the end of that. Gambling days over, case closed.

He tried not to think about T.J., because of the pain it caused. He even felt jealous, because T.J. was with Annie and the others on the boat or somewhere, and they had the benefit of his delightful presence. T.J. was probably happy there. Maybe even better off. But the truth was, he belonged here, on the backstretch. T.J. belonged to his father. Only Billy's own weakness and stupidity and temper had driven him away. First, years ago, it was Annie. Now it was T.J. Would he have nothing at all left in the end?

What if even his fists failed him? So much of what happened with your fists was controlled by your head, and it was his head that had allowed his fists to create this latest disaster.

At least he was grateful that his headache of the morning was gone, as was the burning in his belly after he ran. When he got in shape, the headaches and gutaches would disappear for good. When an athlete let himself get out of shape, he paid a higher price than other people; the body, used to heavy, consistent action, went to hell quicker.

He put She's A Lady back in her stall, tapped her playfully on the nose, and headed for the track.

There was a curious atmosphere to the Hialeah track when the grandstand was empty, when there was nothing moving on the racing turf, when the banners were not flying. Even the birds were quiet.

Billy felt a kind of reverence around him as he leaned against the rail and looked out at the infield, where the pink flamingos and black swans rustled around their nesting areas. The sun was low, limning the palms and pines with gold; the ponds were mirrors.

He felt like he had felt a long time ago when, after his first big bout, he knocked out Perez and became a serious contender for the first time. After all the cheering and congratulations in the dressing room, after the press was gone, after his bruises were attended and he had showered and dressed, after everyone had left the arena, he went back inside to the ring.

He remembered the awe he felt, standing alone in the center of that ring, surrounded by empty seats from which the full house had roared its support while Billy did his fine number on Perez; he remembered the awe he felt at that moment, standing there alone, awe he had not felt when he had first entered the ring for the fight, or even at the end of the fight, when he stood with both gloves raised high, and Perez lay with his head on the bottom strand of ropes.

The awe was in the emptiness, when he realized how much space the crowd had filled, how much attention had been focused on him. The vast sea of empty seats told him how much it all meant.

Hialeah was like that—empty. For a long time he leaned against the rail, watching the nesting birds, watching the lengthening shadows. So many scenes and events wafted through his head: his childhood work and gambling and fights; his first girl friends; his first real amateur bouts and the early professional ones; his final sad and confusing defeat, which stripped him of not only the title but so much more. But nothing stuck in his mind for long. He just stood and mused and looked out across the track.

But then there was a new feeling. He raised his head. Maybe there was some revealing sound or movement or something, but it was almost as if he could feel eyes on him. He turned around.

Many rows up in the grandstand, T.J. was seated in one of the green wicker chairs, looking down at him. One of the huge chandeliers above the first tier seemed to sit on his head like a halo.

Billy was too stunned to do anything but turn away. He looked across the track for a few seconds. Then, jamming his hands casually into his back pockets, and without looking at T.J., he started leisurely climbing the stairs.

T.J. didn't look at him either, not directly. He just sat there, staring out, regarding Billy's progress upwards out of the corner of his eye. He wondered if the Champ would stop, maybe talk to him, or whether he would just continue walking up past him. He didn't even know what he would say if the Champ *did* stop. He sat tensely and swallowed hard.

Billy reached T.J.'s row, started to take another step up, then stopped. Lips puckered in a silent whistle, he slid into T.J.'s row and dropped into the chair right beside him.

Neither looked at the other. Billy whistled a light tune, T.J. pinched his lips together. They both stared out at the track.

Then, still without looking at T.J., Billy said softly, "You know what you are?"

There was a pause, then T.J. answered just as softly, "A pain in the butt?"

Another pause.

"Right." Billy whistled for a few seconds. "And you know what else you are?"

T.J. didn't answer.

"You are the *son* of a pain in the butt. And you know—"

But suddenly T.J. was upon him, nearly strangling him in a hug, tears pouring off T.J.'s face and running

39

down Billy's own, soon mixing with Billy's tears to flood his neck and chest.

Billy grabbed him and pulled his face against his own, patting the back of his blond head. Through clenched teeth, Billy said, "*Never*, I swear to God, *never again! Never* do I let you go, T.J.!"

And T.J. sobbed back, "I ain't gonna leave you, Champ! I ain't never gonna leave you again!"

For a long time father and son held each other, swaying back and forth together in the awesome emptiness of the great grandstand, promising each other in a hundred variations of language and tone that neither would ever leave the other or let the other leave, not ever.

CHAPTER 7

Billy awoke to the soft sound and thought it was the rain beating down on the backstretch. He lay staring at the ceiling, listening to the rain. He thought maybe it was just his own internal clock telling him it was time for roadwork. He checked his watch. No, still the middle of the night.

Then it came again, the soft, whispered call, "Billy?"

He slid out of bed and went to the open window and leaned out over the wet sill. One of the trainers was down there, barely outlined in the dark.

"Billy, someone down here to see you."

Billy started to ask who, then glanced over at the sleeping T.J., and just nodded to the man.

He hurriedly pulled on his pants, tucked his T-shirt inside, and planted his cap. He closed the door quietly behind him and went lightly down the steps. He hunched his shoulders in the rain and plodded through the puddles to one of the barns from which streamed light.

He clucked at a couple of curious horses peering out of their stalls and turned into the lighted barn. "You."

"Hi, Billy."

Annie looked lovely, completely incongruous among the bales of hay and straw, as if it weren't a barn in the middle of the night with the rain pouring, as if she were going to afternoon tea.

"What's the matter?" he asked easily, shaking water from his cap. "Josie didn't tell you? He's here. He's okay." Momentarily unsettled by seeing her, he felt pride in being able to say that.

"She told me." Annie stood some distance from him, framed by straw bales that set off her green outfit like golden light. "Look, you wouldn't come to the phone, so—"

"Business. All the time business." He leaned casually against some feed sacks and shoved the cap back on his head. "So what do you want? Spill it."

"We're going back to New York, Mike and I. But, well, first I wanted to talk to you."

"About what?" Billy sensed her nervousness and was glad for it. This was his turf, and he was in control.

"T.J. found out a couple nights ago that he has a mother." She took a cigarette from her purse and put it delicately between her lips. "He's going to need"—remembering about fires, she put the cigarette away—"an explanation."

A sigh fluttered Billy's lips. "I'll handle that. Something like 'She had a little too much to drink, T.J. Broads do strange things. When you're older you'll find out.' Okay?"

"Oh, come on, Billy." She walked slowly over to him as she spoke. "We made a mess of a marriage, we don't have to make a mess of our child."

"He ain't—"

"It happens. God knows there are a million broken marriages, a million—"

"God knows I'm sick of this—"

"Tell him how it was, Billy, how it is."

He eyed her. "How *is* it?"

"I'm not an angel in heaven, Billy. I'm real, I'm

here." She held out a hand as if to touch him, but didn't. "I made a mistake."

"Helluva mistake!"

"But he's got to know about it, he's got to understand what happened. That two people just couldn't—"

"No, no, no!" He stepped back, waving his hands. "Not two people—*one* person. *I could!* You, what about you?" He jabbed his finger at her. "What I tell him happened? That his mother went to Paris to make dresses for fat French broads? Huh?"

"I didn't leave," she said softly. "I was kicked out."

"The door wasn't locked!"

She looked at the floor. "I was frightened, Billy. I couldn't come back." Then she met his eyes. "Remember?"

"Do I *remember!* You picked one helluva night!"

She put a hand over her eyes, then drew it slowly down her face and sighed. "Look, I'll always say I was kicked out, you'll always say I left. Can't we just talk about our son?"

"He'll be okay. T.J.'s a tough kid."

"Tough?" She looked at him incredulously. "Billy, he's just eight years old. You can't just say, 'You've got a mother,' and drop it there."

"He'll be okay, I said, he's fine." He paced around her. "What about me?"

She followed him with her eyes. "You?"

"Yeah, me!" He jabbed his chest with his thumb. "Billy Flynn! Remember? What about *me?*"

She glanced uneasily around, as if afraid somebody else might be listening. "What is it? What do you want?"

"You can always come back."

"What?"

"You heard me. We'll give you a second chance maybe."

"Oh, Billy"—she shook her head and laughed

nervously—"you're really something. People change, time passes." She hesitated, then softened her voice. "I have a husband, Billy. I love him very much."

"Yeah. So what else is new?" He cocked his head and smiled crookedly. "You forget how it was with us?"

For a moment the electricity was there between them, causing her lips to quiver. "Yes, I remember—the good as well as the bad."

"So?" He sat down on a feed bag and studied his scarred hands.

She pinched her lips together, searching for the right words, as she went over and knelt beside him. "Billy, there are different kinds of love. Let's find *our* way. For T.J." He didn't respond. She put a hand on his hair. "Billy?"

"Watch the hand."

"Help T.J. to understand. Maybe I'm just learning how, but I care." She drew her fingers lightly through his hair. "Will you talk to him?"

He shoved her hand away. "You know I don't like broads messin' with my hair."

She dropped her hand into her lap and stared at it. Then slowly she raised her eyes to his. "Will you talk to him, Billy?"

"I'll talk to him."

"For *his* sake."

"I said I'd talk to him!"

She recoiled from his harsh tone. She stood up and backed slowly off a couple of steps, watching him. "Thank you," she said softly.

"It's . . . it's okay." His voice was much more gentle now, almost apologetic, and he waved lightly to her without looking her way. "I'll talk to him. It's okay. Don't worry about it."

He didn't look her way until she was gone in the rain. Then for a while he stared out the broad, dark doorway through which she had gone.

* * *

Riley called Billy to the phone, then discreetly left the office so Billy could talk privately.

"Billy? Charlie Goodman."

"Hey, Charlie."

"We come up with a bout for you."

"Yeah? Who?"

"Roland Bowers."

"Bowers." Billy scratched his head. "That young guy?"

"Yeah."

"Big."

"Hey, Billy, don't worry about it. He's been puffed up, rep's been pushed by some people. He ain't fought nobody worth nothin'. I seen him fight. Slow as an ox. Perfect for you. Forget what you heard."

"I wasn't saying I was afraid of him, Charlie."

"I know, I know. But what I'm saying is he's got a big rep, but he's easy. Be a snap for you. You'll take him like nothin'. But that big rep will help you, make it look like something when you take him out."

"You think he's right, Charlie? For my first time back?"

"Hey, Billy," Goodman chuckled, "would I lead you wrong? He's a tune-up for you, nothing more than that—between you and me. Be a plaything for you."

Billy rubbed his head with the receiver, then put it back to his ear. "I fought a lot of times for you, Charlie."

"Don't you think I know that?"

"Made a lot of money for you."

"For yourself too, don't forget."

"Forgettin' nothin', Charlie. Never. But I ain't been followin' things too close for a while, Charlie. I'm trustin' you on this."

"And you're right, Billy boy, Leave it to me. Bowers

is the guy. You and he'll fill the house. And you'll take him. And between you and me, I already got inside word that when you do, you'll be right in line for a title shot."

"Sounds good."

"It's settled then. We'll sign it up. Uh, by the way, Billy, you gettin' in shape?"

"'Course. Been workin' out for weeks. I'll get right back in the ring, now you got a fight lined up."

"You gotta look good, you know. Everybody'll be watching this."

"I'll look good, Charlie, you know that." Billy watched a fly buzz around the desk, swung a quick right at it, missing. "What numbers you got in mind?"

"Leave all that to me, Billy. Bowers is, uh—I might offer them a little bigger cut than usual, just to lock 'em in, you know. But that'd be because this one is just a tune-up. Take Bowers, then we call the shots next time out."

"How much bigger?"

"Just leave it to me, Billy."

"Quite a bit's gettin' left to you, Charlie."

"Hey, Billy, you doubtin' me?"

Billy thought for a moment. "Just do your job right, Charlie. I'll do mine."

"Done! I'll lock it up, then we'll get the press in."

"And Charlie?"

"Yeah?"

"Make it soon, huh?"

"Absolutely!"

Billy hung up and stood staring at the phone. He had heard that Bowers was big and a puncher. Billy wasn't scared of Bowers. He wasn't scared of any fighter alive. It was time that scared him, time passed and passing. He needed to get back in the ring in a hurry. Feeling his legs and head and fists work in the ring would bring his confidence back. All he needed was to get back to work.

* * *

T.J., on his bicycle with the long handlebars that looked like antlers, met Billy coming back from his roadwork. "Hey, Champ!"

"Hey!" Billy gasped. His sweatsuit was drenched in sweat, even his heavy boots showed a dark brown stain. He waved his fists, each of which held lead-stick weights. He lumbered up to T.J., huffing and puffing and swinging his weighted fists.

T.J. stopped and stradded his bike. "You been gone a long time, Champ."

"Five miles," he panted, "takes—a long—time." He continued rolling his shoulders and stabbing his fists at the air.

"You're really gettin' in *shape*!"

"Yeah. Check this out." He set himself and began throwing short, crisp punches at the air. His words came in staccato bursts in the same rhythm. "Pick 'em out—that one—that one—left, left, right!—who's that? —left, left, right!—who's—"

"Frank Cox!"

"Yeah—Cox—two left jabs—straight right—put him away—Now who's—this?—feint the right—left hook! —Huh?—who's that?—feint the right—left hook!—"

"Perez!"

"Right!—left hook dropped him—on the ropes—All of 'em—Al Handler, bang!—Sweet Bobby Brown, wham!—Finn Pekkanen, boom!—all of 'em!—Nothin' stands—inna way—a the championship!"

"Roland Bowers!" T.J. yelled happily.

"Yeah." Billy stopped for a second. Then he started circling, throwing out quick left jabs. "Bowers." He jabbed and jabbed. Then he threw a right in low, stepped back, and arced a left hook chest high through the air in front of him. "Gone!"

"Bye, bye, Bowers!"

"You got it! Double him up with a right to the ribs, catch him with the hook." Billy dropped his hands to his sides, dangling them loosely, as he continued bouncing on his toes. "Whew! Gettin' it *together*, T.J., gettin' it *together*!"

"How're the legs, Champ?"

"Okay, okay, they're coming along." He looked down at them as he bounced. "Gettin' it back." He rolled his head around, testing his neck, and danced left and right, leaning as if to avoid punches. Sweat dripped off his nose.

"How's the back, Champ?"

"Back's okay—feels good—be no problem—whap, whap, whap"—he tossed out three quick jabs——"*boom!*"—he delivered his fine, tight left hook. "That's all for Roland Bowers. Whew!"

He stopped dancing and punching and strode panting around the bicycle. "I'm ready for the ring, T.J. Ready!"

T.J. beamed with pride and pleasure. "Champ of the world in six months!"

"Big dough," Billy said, punching the air again, "big time—" Then he leaned over to catch his breath. "Eighty grand—There's this house—I gotta buy."

Billy hopped off his bike and lay it down on the road. He took a towel draped on the handlebars and quickly wiped off Billy's face, hair, shoulders, and back. "You're really *sweating*, Champ!"

"Yeah."

"How come I don't sweat like that?"

"When you're older, T.J. It'll come. Whew." Billy walked toward the barns. T.J. stood up his bike and walked along beside him.

"Gonna buy that house," Billy said. "Then we're gonna travel, you and me."

"Yeah!"

"Gonna see the world, huh? Brazil!"

"Brazil!"

"Yeah, my kid and I. Goin' to Brazil, goin' down to watch them senoritas." He swung his hips. "Cha-cha-cha!"

T.J. aped the movement. "Cha-cha-cha!"

"Right! And New York! Yeah, we'll go to New York, you and me. See everything. Just you and me in New York."

"New York!" T.J. waved a fist.

"Don't need nobody but ourselves, right?"

"Right! Just the Champ and T.J.!"

"And I'll really *be* the Champ."

"Champ of the whole *world*!"

"Then maybe we'll buy some horses, some fine horses of our own, and we'll keep 'em here with She's A Lady and everybody'll be working for *us*."

"Yeah! 'Cause nothin's too good for the Champ, right?"

"The Champ and T.J.!"

T.J. cheered, then suddenly stopped and turned serious. "Champ?"

"Yeah?"

"Nobody's as lucky as me."

*　　*　　*

The bus groaned to a stop, the door swung open, and from it stepped a man with a folded newspaper in one hand and a valise in the other. He looked around to get his bearings. He was a sturdy man with thinning gray hair, a square, sturdy face, and a serious expression. He was dressed in a suit of heavier material than is common in Miami. He was from Chicago and his name was Jackie Shroll. He was a trainer of fighters, and he was here to attend a press conference to which he had not been invited.

He asked directions from a cab driver, then set out walking in the direction the cabbie pointed.

At that time, the press conference was already going on. It was in promoter Charlie Goodman's modest office. Present with Goodman were Billy, looking confident and casual; T.J., looking proud; the old cornerman Georgie, looking nervous as always; and a handful of reporters representing Miami's *News* and *Herald*, Mexico City's *El Tribuno*, United Press International, and *The Ring* magazine, some looking interested, some doubtful.

Billy sat on the desk, the reporters on folding chairs. As they questioned Billy, Goodman moved among them, keeping their glasses filled with the best of booze.

"So that guy was nothing special," the elderly man from *The Ring* was saying, "and he slaughters you. You lose the title and retire. Now you're gonna come back, fight as a heavyweight against this mean kid, go ten rounds on thirty-seven-year-old legs?"

"Hold it now," Billy drawled, rocking back and forth. "Couple things. Let's get things straight for the record. Thirty-six. For the record, I'm thirty-six." The reporters scribbled. "And on that title fight, I had a bad night. Who don't have one off night?"

"Bad ain't a strong enough word," *The Ring* man said.

"Charlie, where you dig this creep up?"

"Easy, Billy," Charlie said, waving a whiskey bottle, "just relax."

"I mean it," Billy went on, eyeing the magazine man. "I don't like what he's sayin' here."

"He's kicking around old times, Billy. We're all friends here, we're all in the business."

"Yeah, well let me add a couple things about what

he said. I never got slaughtered, 'cause here I am. I got beat and I retired, that's all. Now here I am back. And on this fight here, I'll be in better shape than my opponent 'cause I'm *always* in better shape than my opponents. I'll be able to go ten. I could go twenty if I had to. But who says it's gonna go ten? I ain't gonna carry him, you know, just to show you guys I got legs. Next question?"

A local reporter waved his pencil. "I just want to say that win or lose this fight you were the best I ever saw."

"Thank you. I ain't gonna lose it."

"I mean it. You were great, the Prince of the Ring we called you. I watched dozens of guys copy Billy Flynn. If you're fifty percent of what you were, we got a helluva fight."

"Well, thank you very much." Billy squirmed a little at the praise. "Appreciate that. But I'm never less than a hundred percent. If I lost something, you won't notice it."

"See?" Goodman said. "We're all gentlemen, we're all friends here." He came over and sat on the edge of the desk and put a hand on Billy's shoulder. "Here you have one of the great light heavies of all time. Now he'll go as a heavyweight. And against him you got the third-ranked—"

"For the record, fifth-ranked," interjected the *Ring* man.

"Jesus, Abe," Goodman said with sarcasm, "why don't you nitpick me here?"

"Just trying to be accurate."

"Well, what is accurate is you got a great fight coming up here. Who's next?"

"In the papers," said the man from *El Tribuno* with a Spanish accent, "Bowers call you an old man. He says the old man going to the hospital."

Billy chuckled roughly. "A little while back, Dickie

McCurdy said the same thing. The way I remember, Dickie ended up in the back of an ambulance himself. That kind of talk I don't mind. I don't fight with my mouth anyway."

"Well, what you *think* of Bowers?" the man persisted.

"I think he's rough and tough, a good fighter with a bright future—except for this time out."

"Did I understand you to say," asked the UPI man, checking his pad, "that you don't expect the fight to go the full ten?"

"I just said it *may* not. But, okay, I'll give you the answer you want. I think he'll fall inside of ten, okay? But I ain't no Ali, now, I ain't pickin' no round. I'm just saying I think I'll knock him out."

"Why didn't you pick an easier opponent," the UPI man went on, "for a kind of tune-up first?"

Billy didn't like the UPI man either. "Hey, I already tuned up for fifteen years as a fighter before I retired temporarily. I never got *outta* tune."

"Speaking of that," it was still the UPI man, "could I ask you about your last fight?"

"What about it?" Billy glared at him.

"Well, it seemed strange to a lot of people, and you've never spoken publicly about it. You were handling him good for five rounds, then in the sixth you just seemed to fall apart."

"You got hit with that right hand, you'd fall apart too."

"But why all of a—"

"I got hit, that's all! Next?"

"Could you tell us all," put in a local man cautiously, gesturing to include all the reporters as if not daring to ask the question alone, "why you never sought a rematch, even though you were in your prime?"

"Because I retired."

"That's no answer," said the UPI man gruffly.

"That's *my* answer, buster," Billy growled, leaning forward. "No more questions about what happened seven years ago."

"Now Billy—" Goodman looked nervously around. "Next?"

"Is it true," another local man asked, "that you're going as a heavyweight because you couldn't make the one seventy-five limit for a light heavy?"

"No, it is not true. I'm just comfortable at this weight, that's all. I feel good about one eighty-two, one eighty-three. I already won the light-heavyweight championship once. Heavyweight is the top. That's what I'm after."

"And he's not just talking for the press, gentlemen," Goodman put in quickly, trying to ease the tension in the room. He pridefully patted Billy's back. "Believe me, he means it. In a week I'll be selling standing room for this first fight on his comeback trail. No more questions?"

Nobody responded.

"In that case, gentlemen"—Goodman moved toward the door—"everyone downstairs to the deli—sandwiches are on me!"

He ushered them grandly out into the small hallway, where they crowded and bumped into each other before straightening out and walking toward the stairs.

Goodman fell behind and sidled up to Billy. "Hey," he whispered, "you gotta be more *positive* with these guys. They're our *friends*. We *need* them, Billy."

"I don't need nobody to help me fight, Charlie."

"But Billy," he whined, "that ain't a good *attitude*."

"They can wipe their noses with my attitude. I'll show 'em in the ring."

Then, coming down the hallway toward them, Billy saw Jackie Shroll.

"Jackie!" Billy ran up to the trainer, threw an arm

around him, and steered him away from Goodman and the press. "Hey, am I glad to see you!"

"Yeah, sure, Billy. That's why you never called me."

"I was gonna, Jackie, honest . . ."

Shortly thereafter they were seated in a booth at the coffee shop downstairs. They nibbled at club sandwiches.

"Of course I'm hurt as hell," Jackie said. "But that don't matter. Here you get a big fight, no phone call."

"I really *was* gonna call you. But I figure, why waste your time, my time, when the fight isn't even signed?"

"Sure, Billy."

"Truth! I swear!" Billy raised his right hand. "I was gonna call you tomorrow. We just signed today."

"Hey, Billy, never throw bull at an old bull-thrower." Jackie smiled wryly. "You been working out, sparring, getting everything set. That's when you need a trainer, right?" He leaned across the table. "You don't call because you figure Jackie might cause a problem, eh?"

"What problem?" Billy held his palms up.

"Jackie might just go to the medical examiner, right?"

"What you talkin' about?"

Jackie snorted and leaned back, turning sideways in the booth and crossing his legs. "You don't think I know?" Abruptly he leaned back across the table again. "Listen, seven years ago a bum that couldn't carry your shoes takes you apart. All of a sudden."

Billy grimaced and rubbed his belly. "I never felt right, that fight. Something I ate or something."

"Bull."

"Wasn't lookin' for that right—"

"Hey!" Jackie's voice became a whisper, at once angry and friendly and confidential. "This is Jackie sittin' here, Billy. This ain't some half-baked, punch-drunk trainer you're talking to. You think Jackie don't know? You think Jackie don't know *you?*" He shoved his sandwich away. "You took too many punches that night."

"Punches didn't bother me none."

"No, huh?"

"Lotta small things . . ."

"Knocked you out, is what they did. And they bothered *me*. Yeah, they sure as hell bothered Jackie, those shots." He nodded briskly. "So then afterwards, later on, we sit down and talk, remember? And you say maybe it's over. And actually I don't feel bad about that. Sure, I act sad, show you I'm sad, but inside I'm happy for you, Billy."

"Happy I quit?"

"Yeah, that's right, believe it or not. 'Cause o' those shots you took. 'Cause o' the way the whole thing went down. And 'cause we had enough." Jackie rubbed his chin and looked off. "We did it all, Billy, we had our times. Then we shook hands, and I said to you, 'What's it gonna be, Billy?' Remember me asking that? I said, 'We got eight grand in the kitty, how about a nice little bar? Nothin' fancy, but you put our name over the door. You got friends, make it a nice, quiet business.'"

"I remember." Billy fingered his sandwich.

"But you wanted the track, right? For the boy. Fresh air, clean environment, nothing wrong with that, long as you stay away from the betting windows. You don't get rich, but it ain't bad. I said it then, I'm saying it now."

"Meaning?"

"Meaning it's *crazy*, Billy, this whole thing is a big mistake. It ain't like you're going back on the *stage* or something like some old actor. You're talking about the *ring*. You're talking about getting *hit!*"

"Hey, I'm in great shape, Jackie." Billy smiled and spread his arms. "I'm workin' hard, feelin' great. I ain't felt this strong in years."

Jackie peered at him. Then slowly he brought up his arm and tapped the heel of his hand against his forehead. "Headaches."

"What?"

Suddenly he reached across to Billy's shirt pocket, pulled out the tin of aspirin, and tossed it onto the table. He never took his eyes off Billy's. "You still getting 'em?"

"So who doesn't get a headache now and then?"

"No Billy, that ain't what we're talking about."

"Even you must get—"

"You know what headaches I'm talking about!" He flicked the aspirin tin toward Billy with his finger, still eyeing him. He softened his voice. "You still getting 'em?"

Billy looked thoughtful and rubbed his belly. "Actually, I get more pains in my—"

"The headaches, Billy. This is Jackie here asking. Nobody else knows nothing. Just us. Tell me."

Billy's face turned somber. Pretenses were gone. There was no fooling Jackie, never had been. There were more famous trainers in the business, but none better, from Billy's view. Jackie had guided him to the championship. But more important, Jackie had been there through the early going, when Billy was learning the ropes, when nobody knew how good he could become. Jackie had made sure he was brought along carefully, no crazy fights just for a quick buck. And Jackie had watched over other things too—which people were allowed to hang around and which hustlers were not, how the purses got divided up, how Billy spent his money. All this plus being in his corner for every fight as a pro. Besides T.J., Jackie had been the most important guy in his life.

Billy looked at the table. "I gotta take this shot. For me and my kid. Nobody stops me. I'm takin' this fight."

Jackie sighed through clenched teeth and slumped back in the seat. "Comeback fight," he muttered, "what a stupid—"

"With you or without you," Billy said firmly, "it don't matter. My mind's made up."

Jackie pinched his eyes with his thumb and forefinger. "Of all the stupid, punch-drunk, half-baked ideas . . ."

"With you or without you, Jackie."

Jackie reached for his sandwich, jammed it between his teeth, and chomped down fiercely. "I'd have to be —" he mumbled between chews, "crazy myself—to—"

"I need you, Jackie." Suddenly Billy found himself pleading. Half-rising out of his seat, he leaned across the table to take Jackie's shoulder. "Jackie, I need you with me!"

Jackie glanced at him and looked away. Then he glanced at him a little longer, and looked away again. When he faced him the third time, he said, "Okay." He sighed and nodded. "I'm with you Billy."

* * *

When Jackie got to the gym, the two fighters were already sparring. The tiers of folding chairs on two sides of the ring were filled. Jackie leaned back against the wall to watch.

The black fighter was of no interest to Jackie; the white one was. That was Roland Bowers. Bowers was coming in with savage intensity, growling through his mouthpiece, slamming punches to the body, taking several light jabs in return without flinching, digging more punches into the midsection, and then delivering his explosive right uppercut that sent the black fighter reeling against the ropes. With his man pinned there, Bowers hammered at him with both hands, butchering him until somebody called time. A handler jumped into the ring to pull Bowers away. The black fighter was out on his feet.

Jackie watched all this closely. Bowers was tough all right. Rough as hell. Carried that right like an Apache with a war club. That right hand was all he had heard it was. Devastating to the body. Uppercut like a bomb. Take your head off. And he was hungry too. You could see that in his eyes and his style. He was murderous. He didn't mind getting hit. He would take everything you threw in order to move in on you and deliver that right. He would be champion one day.

But not yet. It was Jackie's job to see that he didn't walk over Billy Flynn on his way to the title. Jackie didn't know how many fights Billy had left in him, but he always took them one at a time, and this one was next. Roland Bowers. What a damned toughie Billy had picked for his first step back. Jackie would have picked an easier one first, somebody who would pressure Billy just enough to make him fight, allow him to get his timing and confidence back.

But Bowers wasn't perfect. He had faults. He was young and he would learn. But seven years ago Billy would have cleaned him good, maybe knocked him out early. Because Billy moved so well and set himself so quickly and could deliver as clean a knockout as anybody in the business. Or Billy could stick and move all night long if necessary to win a decision. Seven years ago Billy would have slipped those powerful but clumsy right hands, jabbed Bowers crazy, and cold-cocked him when he ducked that big head.

Seven years ago it would have been like that. Jackie didn't know just how it would be now. Billy was looking pretty good in the ring, had good power, moved pretty well. But you never really knew what seven years took out of your stamina and speed until the fight itself. You never knew if a fighter would run out of gas until you saw him in the ring against somebody who was applying real pressure, really trying to hurt you, where a single mistake could get you knocked out or change the course of the fight.

Another thing you never knew before your fighter was in the ring for real was just how much of a punch he could take. The sparring ring didn't give you the answer to that. But Bowers would pose the question sure enough—he could punch like hell.

"Pit bull," Jackie mumbled to himself as he turned to go. "The guy's like a fighting dog, a pit bull, like he's trained to go for the kill and fight to the death."

* * *

"Watch him now, watch him while he comes in." Jackie pointed to the flickering images on the wall of his hotel room as he ran the film of Bowers's most recent fight. Billy sat on the edge of the bed peering at the scene.

"Hardly no jab at all, like he doesn't want to waste no time," Jackie said. "Comes right in low to the body . . . See? . . . see? . . . Now against the ropes, again those big body shots . . . there! . . . there! . . . Now the guy's trying to fight his way off the ropes by sticking that jab in Bowers's face. But Bowers is pretty good at slipping those . . . see? . . . not bad at all in slipping those. You got to get away from the ropes against him . . . Now watch."

In the film, Bowers continued working his man over against the ropes, then stepped back slightly and delivered that fierce right uppercut, catching his opponent square under the chin and dropping him.

The film ended and Jackie lit a cigarette. "I checked the other films but we got all we need right here."

"Guy's tough," Billy said, reaching for his coffee cup.

"Yeah, no doubt about it."

"So what do I fight him with?"

Jackie puffed out a smoke ring, thought for a moment, then put his cigarette on the ashtray and stood up in the middle of the room. "I seen it. The flaw. You didn't catch it?"

"Maybe. What'd you see?"

Jackie picked up the cigarette and stuck it in the corner of his mouth. He assumed a boxer's stance. "Okay. He comes with that little pawing jab of his, *pfff, pfff*—he flicked out light jabs. "But they don't mean nothing. He's just measuring you, looking to pop the right. So behind that jab, *pfff, pfff*, he works downstairs, both hands to the body, bam—bam—" He slammed his imaginary opponent in the midsection. "Now, you ain't gonna be able to slip all those. Gonna have to take a couple, 'cause you don't dare cover up completely. 'Cause he's still looking to pop that right, that uppercut. Okay, so now he's in there, working low, and you're moving, like a snake in there, slipping some and taking some. And he's getting ready to unload, but what does he do?"

Billy said nothing, just watched closely and listened.

"Here's what he does" Jackie dipped his right shoulder slightly while cocking his right hand for an uppercut. "He telegraphs it. About an inch he drops it, like a baseball player with a hitch in his swing. And for that split second he's open, Billy. While he's loading up that right, he's open—"

"For the left hook." Billy nodded.

"You got it, baby! You seen it too!" Jackie flashed a mean grin. "Reminds me so much of Frazier against Ali. Frazier was setting up Ali the same way—waiting for that Ali right uppercut that left Ali open for the left hook. And Frazier had the best left hook in the business. Only difference was speed. It's like it was reversed. Frazier didn't have your speed, and Bowers doesn't have Ali's. And right now you got the best left hook God created, Billy. When Bowers loads up that uppercut, you're gonna hook, and you're gonna knock this animal down, Billy!"

"You figure?"

"Hey, if you got fifty percent left from what you had, you can drop him. Absolutely. That's how you win this fight."

Billy picked up a sheaf of photographs of Bowers in action and leafed through them. He stopped at one, a closeup of Bowers's scowling face. His dark hair matted over his forehead gave the look added menace. "Guy sure looks like he means business."

"Forget how he looks," Jackie said, snatching the picture out of Billy's hands. "Ugly don't win fights. He's just a fighter. A fighter with a flaw."

"Yeah." Billy pursed his lips and stared at the wall. "I'm gonna win this fight."

Jackie locked his arm around Billy's head. "*We're* gonna win this fight, Billy boy. Oh, yeah!"

CHAPTER 8

T.J. was embarrassed to bring the letter to Josie because she might think her tutoring was being wasted.

"I really tried," he said, "but I just can't figure it out."

"Nothing unusual about that, T.J.," she said while retying her pony tail with its pink ribbon. "Handwritten letters can be difficult for anybody to decipher."

"What's that? Deci—"

"Decipher? Figure out. And I can see where this one would be hard to read." She scanned the letter quickly, then began to read aloud: " 'Dear Timmy: Thank you for the wonderful time we had together the other day. Mike and I both enjoyed you so much. I'm sorry you decided not to come with us to New York, but I understand. I miss you, and I can only hope that you'll remember that each day I stop a hundred times to think of you.' "

"A hundred?"

"That's what she says here. 'Mike says to send a special hello. Here in New York it's dark and rainy outside. I remember you in sunshine and that makes me feel better. Know that I love you. Annie.' "

She handed T.J. the letter and he stuffed it carelessly into his shirt pocket. She watched his face and knew that he was concerned about what Annie had told him the other day. "T.J.," she said, picking her words cautiously, "women, when they're frightened, sometimes they do crazy things without even realizing it. Like a scared horse that runs into a fence instead of jumping over it. Later, when they look back, they can see the mistakes, and they want to make up for it."

"Are women different that way?"

"From men? Well, I really don't know. But I'm a woman, and Annie's a woman, and I think maybe I can tell something about what's going on with her, what went on, how she feels."

"You think Annie was scared?"

"Maybe something like that."

"But why? What of?"

"Scared of the truth, maybe. Scared of losing something she loves. Even scared of loving. Love scares people sometimes." She studied T.J.'s downcast eyes. "Why don't you write to her?" She smiled at him. "I'll help you. We'll sit down and do it together. A letter from you would make her very happy."

"I gotta find the Champ." T.J. began walking away. "Thanks for reading it to me, Josie."

"Sure. Uh, T.J.? The letter, I wouldn't show it to the Champ right now. It might make him upset."

T.J. stopped and put his hand to the pocket containing the letter. "But I always tell him everything."

"Just once, zip the lip." She drew her thumb and forefinger across her lips. "Okay? He's already got a lot on his mind. Okay?"

"Well, okay."

* * *

Billy felt his concentration coming back. His quick fists beat a tattoo on the dangling peanut bag, rattling it back against its support with steady, sure rhythm. He had forgotten how difficult it was to concentrate, how important it was, how long it took for fine tuning. But as his fists worked against the bag in fast, even tempo, he found his mind drifting less and less, and was able to focus more and more clearly on the work of his hands.

He finished with the speed bag and stepped in front of the full length mirror. He shadow boxed for a while, bobbing and weaving, snapping out short punches at his image, keeping his weight on the balls of his feet as he danced. He felt good, thought he looked good too. The target he was looking at in the mirror would not be easy to hit.

"Okay, Billy," Jackie called, "let's go in the ring!"

Billy donned his headguard and protective belt and climbed through the ropes. His opponent for today's workout was a chunky black heavyweight who had once worked with Bowers and knew that fighter's style.

Jackie leaned over the ropes to watch. Georgie stood on the floor and leaned on the ring apron with his elbows. Next to him stood T.J., his head just even with the mat. Several other fighters interrupted their training to come over and watch. Hesh was across from Jackie manning the bell. He banged the hammer against the car wheel, and the fighters went to work.

The black fighter came boring in, Billy dancing away on his toes, circling and jabbing. His fast left jab popped off the headguard, snapping the other man's head back. Billy slid under a right and answered with a right of his own. As Jackie had instructed him, Billy circled continually away from his sparring partner's right hand, and kept his left jab busy on the man's head.

They worked four quick rounds, Billy loosening up more each round, dancing and jabbing, occasionally snapping out the right.

In the fifth, his opponent began seriously working to the body. Billy caught some of the punches with his elbows, took others in the gut. Jackie watched

Billy's face closely for signs of the effects of those body shots. He seemed to be taking them well.

"What you think?" Georgie asked Jackie.

"I think they hurt," Jackie said, "but he looks okay."

In the sixth round Billy opened up. He was really working hard now, concentrating intensely, sweat spraying off his head as he circled and jabbed. He stepped inside of another right and dug a left to the body. As the sparmate bulled him into the ropes, Billy feinted left and right with his head, slipping the punches and causing the fighter to lunge awkwardly past him into the ropes.

"Wowee!" Georgie sang, slapping the mat. "He head-feints him outta his shoes!"

"Yeah, but that ain't Bowers in there," Jackie said. "Mr. Bowers, I don't think a couple head feints is gonna bother him much." He cupped his hands around his mouth to call: "Fifteen seconds, Billy! Combinations! Finish it up!"

"Open up on him now, Champ!" cried T.J. "Work out there, Champ!"

Billy, circling to his right, suddenly stopped, planted his feet, and fired out a right that bounced off the man's temple. Then he feinted to his left, cleverly slipped the right uppercut, and hooked a fierce left to the man's jaw, straightening him up. Two quick left jabs in a blur, a straight right, and again the left hook on the ear. The man sagged back against the ropes and covered up.

Hesh rang the bell to end it.

"Way to work, Billy!" Georgie called up happily.

"Okay, that's it," Jackie said. "Get your rubdown, Billy."

Billy came over to lean across the ropes, panting. "I feel great—Could go—two more rounds—easy—I'm just—workin' up a sweat."

"Six rounds," Jackie said, tossing him a towel, "that's enough. Tomorrow you do eight."

"Terrific, Billy!" Georgie said, climbing into the ring to help him towel off "Just terrific!"

"Yeah." Billy lifted the top strand of rope and ducked under and jumped down from the ring. "Yeah, I was okay."

"They never could touch him, Jackie," Georgie chortled, "and they still can't!"

"He's coming along," Jackie said more soberly. "He's gettin' there."

Other fighters now muttered their approval and nodded to Billy.

"I really could go more, Jackie," Billy said as they walked toward the locker room.

"If there's one thing I know," Jackie said, "it's how to pace a fighter. The idea is not to be ready today or tomorrow. Fight time, that's when you're ready."

"Yeah."

A couple of men in leisure suits leaned against the wall watching the fighters walk out.

"He's still cute," said one of them in a low voice. "You gotta admit that."

"Bowers eats up cute fighters," said the other. "Fourth round, damn jackhammer right. Poor Billy'll be stretched out, his leg twitching. We'll put it all on Bowers, every penny."

"You're so sure?"

"What I make on fights last year, half a mill? Sure I'm sure. One thing I can't figure out."

"What's that?"

"Why's he doing this? Why's Flynn trying to do this?"

T.J., lagging behind the exiting fighters, and for his size unnoticed by the two gamblers, wished he hadn't heard this dialogue. Now he ducked his head and hurried by them toward the locker room. He knew that this was something he could never tell the Champ, because it would bother him. Yet it bothered T.J. too, and deeply, and he wished he hadn't heard it and wouldn't have to keep it inside him where it hurt.

* * *

Josie and Beau struggled to calm a newly arrived horse that had been spooked by the barking of a dog.

"Hold her now!" Beau called, pulling on his rope. "Take in on it now!"

Josie drew her rope tight on the other side, completing the double noose on the horse's neck. "Easy, girl, easy!"

"Back off, T.J.!" Beau yelled, motioning T.J. away with one hand. "She can kick!"

T.J. backed off and watched anxiously. "You ain't hurting her, are you? Are you hurting her?"

"No, no," Beau said, sliding his hands up the rope to get nearer to the scared horse. "We ain't hurtin' her none. Horse got a neck like a tree. See? She's already comin' around."

Josie had inched close enough to pat the snorting mare's neck, and that had a calming effect.

"Go ahead now, Josie," Beau said, nodding. "I got her."

While Beau held the rope taut, Josie patted the mare's neck, stroked it, finally nuzzled it. She hopped out of the way when the horse bobbed its head hard, then moved back in again to pat her.

"Okay," Beau said, "we'll just move her now." He began walking the horse in a slow circle while Josie caressed its neck. "She's fine, gonna be real fine."

"How come this horse got so scared," T.J. asked, "when the other horses aren't?"

"Well, you get in a new place," Beau said, "where you ain't used to, and somethin' whoops at your heels, you shy off. Horse ain't no different from you in that regard. 'Cept horses can't talk. But see when you get in a strange place sometime, where you ain't got no friends and ain't nothin' familiar. Dog nips at your heels, see you don't jump. Horse can't say, 'Hey, dog, hush up now!'"

T.J. laughed.

"And you see, horse don't know we're her friends yet. But still we holdin' onto her. And she don't know where that dog is at. So it takes a while for her to settle in. Where you headin', T.J., with that nice clean shirt on?"

"Going to the gym, with Jackie."

"Catch the Champ workin' out?"

"Nope. Another gym. We're gonna see Bowers."

"That a fact? Well," he chuckled, "make sure ain't no dog nip at your heels."

Jackie had finally relented and agreed to let T.J. see Bowers work, though he wasn't entirely happy with the idea. As it turned out, T.J. wasn't prepared for the ferocity he saw in the Champ's upcoming opponent.

They stood near the wall amid a bunch of people watching Bowers work the heavy bag. He didn't dance and snap out punches like the Champ did, he tore into it, flat-footed, as if trying to rip the bag apart. His face was a snarl, and each heavy thud of a fist was accompanied by a primal grunt.

T.J. winced as with growing apprehension he watched Roland Bowers's savage attack on the bag. Until then, Bowers had just been a name, along with words to describe him. Now he was flesh and blood, a large, powerful, ornery antagonist, and his blows to the heavy bag and his facial expressions as he delivered them brought the message home to T.J. loud and clear.

"Can we go now?" he whispered.

"Yeah, okay. Had enough?"

"Yeah." T.J. had already seen Bowers's sparring partner climb into the ring. The man had black hair, but otherwise was built along the lines of the Champ. From watching the Champ spar, he knew what was in store for this man, whose job it would be to emulate the Champ's style for Bowers to beat up on. And he had no stomach for that.

"You okay, T.J.?" Jackie asked as they walked out. T.J. looked pale.

"Yeah." He was scared. Bowers would certainly show up in his dreams. That was okay. What scared him more was what Bowers would be like when he showed up in the ring against the Champ.

"Don't worry, T.J., your old man is one helluva good fighter."

"Yeah? Yeah." He hoped Jackie hadn't caught his doubt. For the first time, T.J. was nervous about the fight. He had thought the Champ invincible, been sure of it. Now he wondered. He tried to force it from his mind.

"You know those shots back there on the bag?" Jackie said.

"Yeah?"

"Your old man can take those."

"Wow," T.J. said softly, feeling both pride and pain.

*　*　*

T.J. jogged alongside as Billy completed his roadwork. He couldn't run far with Billy, but lately had taken to joining him for the last half-mile or so. And today Billy had chosen to run along the ocean, saying he needed "to breathe some good salt air." And they had worn their bathing trunks under their running clothes.

"Hey, Champ," T.J. said, panting, "I was thinking, you know—why do you—want to fight again?" He huffed a few more yards. "I mean, what for?"

39

"What for?" Billy came to a sudden stop and put his hands on his hips and drew in some deep breaths. "What kinda crap is that? Money's what for. The title. You know all the what fors."

"Yeah, but you had the title." T.J. tried to breathe as easily as his father. "And everybody knows you were the Champ. You got nothin' to prove."

Billy eyed him suspiciously. "Hey, wait a minute. Whose camp you in? I think I got me a con man here. Who you been talkin' to?" Before T.J. could answer, Billy started running again. "T.J., you're becoming a strange little kid. I don't understand you anymore. You keep secrets from me. Like Annie's letters!"

T.J. raced to catch up. "You found out?"

" 'Course I found out. I almost break my neck the other day steppin' on that loose board there. Ho boy, I say, T.J.'s beginning to hide stuff on me again."

"No, no, I just—"

"You saw Bowers, huh?"

"Yeah, Jackie—"

"So if you had to put money down today, which fighter you put it on, him or me?"

"You!"

"Hey! You got it!" Billy stopped, gulped some deep breaths of ocean air, then kicked off his shoes and started peeling off his sweatsuit. "Come on, you little chicken! Get them clothes off!"

T.J. quickly pulled off his shirt and flung it aside. "I'm sorry, Champ—about the letter, I mean. You upset?"

"Upset? Me? Nothin' upsets me! Heck no, she can write to you all she wants. Nothing wrong with that. You don't have to hide nothin'." Now clad only in his swim trunks, Billy flexed his shoulders. "You written her back?"

"No."

"You mean no, or you mean not yet?"

"Well—"

"Nothing wrong with that either." He smiled at T.J.

"I'll do it tonight," T.J. said happily, greatly relieved.

"You act like you think I'm an ogre or something sometimes."

"What's a ogre?"

"Ask Josie! It's a little devil, like *you*! Come on, let's hit that water!"

T.J. ran after him. "Hey, Champ? You don't mind that Jackie took me—"

"Lemme ask you something, T.J." Billy stopped on the sand.

"What?"

"You like her?"

"Who?"

"You know who. Annie. You like her?"

"I sure do, Champ!"

Billy grabbed him under the arms and hoisted him up high over his head. Then he swung him down and headed for the water.

"Did ya love her, Champ?" T.J. called, running after.

Splashing into the waves, Billy shouted back, "Course I loved her! I didn't love her, I wouldn't have *you*!"

T.J. tumbled into the waves behind the Champ, and was brought up laughing and coughing in his strong arms.

* * *

The Phillips residence in New York was a lushly furnished five-room apartment overlooking Central Park. The furniture was mostly antiques, polished into deep, rich browns. The draperies pulled across the broad windows were of Scandinavian designs, the subtle, modern sweeps and swirls on the fabric blending nicely with the elegant old chairs and sofas and settees and coffee tables and lamps.

Annie and Mike sprawled on the Oriental carpet on the living room floor playing Monopoly.

"Please, please, dice," Annie prayed, "just one more time." She shook the dice and rolled them out.

"Right onto Boardwalk," Mike said, moving her piece. "And I've got a hotel on it. Pay up."

"Drat!" She sat up and put her hands on her knees. "I can't. Look, I'll give you a thousand and a free ride on the yellows."

"Pay up. Game's over."

Playfully she flipped over the board, scattering the pieces and money and houses and hotels all over the rug. Then she sat back on her haunches pretending to sulk. "I don't believe it. I'm zero for fifty. I'll never beat you, never in my mortal life." She got up and walked away into the dining room.

Mike came up behind and put his arms around her. "You've been nervous as all getout the whole evening," he said softly. "What's wrong?"

"Sorry, I didn't mean for it to show." She turned toward him and put her hands on his shoulders. "I got a letter from T.J. today. My first letter from my son." She smiled wanly.

"Hey, that's great," Mike smiled back, "that's terrific. So how's T.J.?"

"He's fine. It's Billy. Billy's making a comeback."

"But . . . but that's crazy." Mike released her and leaned back, looking at her. "It's crazy. Are you certain?"

"Yup. T.J. spells out details. He's even seen him spar in the ring."

"But why would he do it? What's he trying to prove?"

"Maybe it has to do with me." She walked back

to the living room and sat on a couch, curling her legs under her. Mike followed. "And you can guess what it is, Mike, what he's trying to prove. He might be saying, 'Look, T.J., this is your father here. She may have the dough, but I'm the Champ. Champion of the world. Let me show you how it was, T.J.' Could be something like that."

"You really think that's it?"

"Probably."

Mike pondered a moment, pacing on the rug. "Every fighter dreams of making a comeback."

"Maybe so. But in this case—well, take me out of the picture, put things back the way they were, and what've you got?"

"I think you're putting a ridiculous burden on yourself. Maybe he just wants to hold the title again, have the glory *and* the dough like it was before. That could be enough of a lure in itself."

"Whatever." She picked idly at the nap of the sofa, looking at her fingers. "In any case, I think I should be there—for T.J. So I've decided to go. This Thursday in Miami."

Mike stopped short, his back to her.

"Does that bother you?"

"Yes." He half-turned his head. "Yes, it does. But I wouldn't ask you not to. You know that."

"Yes, I do." She slid off the sofa and walked up behind him and put her arms around his chest. "That's why I love you."

He gave a short chuckle. "Well, I'm glad for that. In any case, well, give me a call if you decide to stay there and walk horses for a living."

Annie laughed with a lightness to match his words. But his words weren't entirely empty. It was difficult for him, of course, knowing she would be going down there to watch her former husband. It would be even more difficult for her. She really *was* doing it for T.J. T.J. had asked her to come.

* * *

In recent weeks Billy had seldom been at the backstretch, having moved into a room next to Jackie's and concentrated on training in the gym. T.J. was with him most of the time.

On fight day they visited the backstretch. T.J. at his heels, Billy walked into the office, his hand full of free tickets.

"For you, Mr. Riley, and for Mrs. Riley. Good seats too."

"Thanks, Billy," Riley said, taking the tickets. "We're really looking forward to it. Billy?" Riley looked at him earnestly.

"Yeah?"

"I just want you to know that you always have your job here, if you want it. I mean, we don't expect you'll *need* it, since you're gonna win and go on for the title and be a full-time fighter again."

"Well, I hope so." Billy was growing edgy. "Well, I gotta be—"

"But just in case, Billy." Riley stuck out his hand and Billy shook it. "Champ or not, we're always your friends here. And we wanna see you from time to time."

"Absolutely. Well, so long."

He found Beau and held out a ticket. "You'll be comin' tonight, won't you, Beau?"

"No, I ain't, Billy, I ain't, if you don't mind." Beau shook his head slowly. "Fightin' ain't got too many good memories for me, I guess. And if I was there, I'd just be nearly feelin' what *you* felt, and gettin' all my juices in a uproar. If you don't take offense, I'd just rather not. Too far along for that kinda

197

excitement, I guess. You understand me, Billy?" He looked hard into Billy's eyes.

"Okay. Sure, Beau, I understand."

"But I ain't no less behind you, pullin' for you, prayin' for you—understand that too. And I want to hear all about it, later on, blow by blow!"

"You got it!"

"And you won't forget us now, we your *friends* here!"

"I ain't forgettin' nothin'!" Billy said, shaking the old man's hand warmly. "And T.J. here, he ain't forgettin' neither. He'll be around. Still got his horse here about ready to race again. And maybe we'll be bringin' in some more, just to keep you company."

"Yeah!" T.J. added brightly. "And keep the dogs away from 'em!"

"Oh, yes, yes, yes," Beau said, grinning and mussing T.J.'s hair.

Before they left, Josie came up to give Billy a warm kiss and whisper in his ear, "You'll be coming by from time to time?"

"What *you* think?" he said, grinning slyly.

"Luck, huh?" She blew him another kiss.

Then he and T.J. drove off, wind whipping their hair in the open convertible.

"Why didn't Beau wanna come?" T.J. asked. "I didn't really understand all that."

"Dunno. Don't matter."

"You okay, Champ? You upset?"

"I'm fine! Don't bother me now! From now on, don't bother me! I gotta think about the fight, from now on!"

T.J. faced front. "I'm sorry, Champ," he said softly.

"Hey!" Billy, smiling, reached over and ruffled T.J.'s hair. "Don't go sad on me now, okay? Everything's gonna be fine. I just gotta concentrate on the fight, okay?"

"Sure, Champ!" T.J. was happy again. "I'm gonna concentrate on it too!"

*　*　*

They entered through the back door into a narrow concrete corridor where the old green paint was peeling off. Graffiti, in both English and Spanish, marred the fading walls; but that went unnoticed. Jackie led the way, carrying a valise containing Billy's shoes, socks, trunks, and three mouthpieces. Then came Hesh, under his arm a paper bag in which were other odd bits of the fighter's paraphernalia.

Then came Billy, his arm on T.J.'s shoulder. Like the others, Billy was wearing a simple sport shirt and slacks. Unlike the others, his face had the stubble of three days' growth of beard—for luck, he had told T.J. Draped over T.J.'s arm was the black silk robe with white lettering: BILLY FLYNN—THE CHAMP.

Bringing up the rear of this somber procession was Georgie, his shabby little satchel filled with salves and styptics and Q-Tips and all the things a cut man needs in the corner.

They could hear above them the noise of the crowd cheering a preliminary bout. The building seemed to shudder from it.

They turned a corner. Ahead, leaning against a wall and wearing a well-tailored, dapper, stylish brown suit, was Bowers. He was talking animatedly to a small, paunchy man in a T-shirt; and, as he gestured, several large rings flashed on his fingers.

Billy looked grimly at his opponent as they neared him. Then Bowers abruptly broke off his conversation, looked up, and he and Billy exchanged brief, barely perceptible nods.

When they passed, T.J. started to look back. Billy put a hand on his neck to keep him facing forward.

At the door to their dressing room—a battered

green portal that looked like somebody had tried to kick it in—the uniformed cop stepped aside for them to enter.

Their dressing room was grimy and small, with bits of dirty adhesive tape and used gauze littering the floor, stains on the walls, and an old rubbing table. Altogether, the room, T.J. thought, was not befitting the Champ. But he didn't say anything. The Champ had his mind on the fight and didn't seem to notice the demeaning surroundings.

A moment later, the inspector from the boxing commission came in, nodded silently to everybody, and said to Jackie, "Okay, go ahead."

Billy quickly stripped down, pulled on his boxing trunks, and sat on the rubbing table. Jackie went to work taping his hands. The inspector watched. So did T.J. Over in the corner at a small table, Georgie and Hesh pulled equipment out of their bags and sorted it and checked it out. Then they too watched as Jackie completed the taping.

The inspector initialed the taping on both hands with a felt-tip pen, nodded, and left without speaking.

As he left, the suction from the closing door pulled another door slightly open, the door between the dressing rooms. Through that small opening, Billy and Bowers saw each other again for a few seconds. No scowls passed between them; they exchanged only brief looks of mutual understanding—two fighters about to go to work on each other.

"Hesh," Jackie said softly, "get the door."

Hesh closed the door, making sure this time it was locked.

Charlie Goodman came in, all smiles and puffed-up chest, his cigar waggling in his lips. "I seen it out there, gentlemen, but I don't believe it! Gentlemen, this is a one-hundred-percent jam-packed sellout crowd!" He tapped Billy's arm. "Good luck out there, Billy. I really mean that."

Billy stared through him as if he weren't there.

T.J., feeling the tension in the room, slunk back against the wall to be out of the way. Goodman, feeling it, backed uncomfortably out of the room, nodding his good-byes.

Billy slid off the table, flexed his bandaged hands, and went over to stand before the mirror. He began dancing on his toes, flicking out left jabs, then rights, dancing with his reflection, punching at the air, his breath coming in low grunts with the punches. Everybody in the room watched him silently. No one wanted to disturb these precious moments of Billy's concentration, when he was in his own separate world, feeling his muscles loosen, feeling the tempo of his heart pick up, feeling the sweat surface and run down his stubbled chin and under his arms. It was this final time when Billy prepared himself, pumped himself up with adrenalin, got his mind in tune with his hands and feet by watching himself dance and punch the air.

T.J. stood transfixed against the opposite wall, his mouth hanging open. Somehow this was awesome to him, how Billy was shadowboxing and dancing and staring at himself without blinking, and how everybody who would be in his corner was watching him, not talking, just standing there focusing all attention on the Champ. It made the Champ the largest figure in the whole world. It was almost scary, how intense the Champ was, and how everybody just stood there watching his every move as if he were God.

Lowly then, so lowly at first that T.J. didn't hear it, Jackie was talking to Billy. "Jab . . . snap it in . . . that's right . . . He's coming at you . . . in the corner, Billy, grab the shoulder and spin out . . ."

Billy smoothly went into the motions as directed, jabbing, slipping out of the corner.

"Now, Billy, string out the combinations . . . You got him, he's off balance . . . That's right . . . let him come to you, let him come . . ."

Billy's hands were flashing, darting out, as he danced and circled and feinted.

"You're movin' away, Billy . . . He's got blood in the corner of his left eye . . . reach for it . . . That's it, bust him open . . . He's cocking the right, Billy . . . Now!"

Billy hooked the left savagely, then raised both fists.

"That's my boy, Billy!" Jackie crowed, putting an arm around him. "That's my wonder boy!"

Everybody smiled and nodded with the break in tension.

Then the buzzer sounded in the room. Smiles disappeared. Everybody except Billy froze. Billy continued dancing on his toes, facing the door. Then Georgie picked up his satchel and bucket, Hesh threw a bunch of towels over his shoulder, and Jackie stepped in front of Billy.

He grabbed Billy by the biceps and peered into his eyes. "Okay, Billy, you're ready. Right on time. Just like I told you. You're ready to win this fight."

Billy stopped bouncing. He turned to T.J. and said his first words since entering the building. "T.J., gimme the robe."

T.J. snatched it from the table and handed it to him.

Billy tossed it around his shoulders. Then he grabbed T.J. in his taped hands, picked him up, hugged him tight, and put him back down.

"Let's go," Billy said.

CHAPTER 9

When they entered the main arena floor, they were met by the roar of a crowd already on its feet, whipped up by the prior appearance of Roland Bowers, and it was bellowing its approval or disapproval of the younger fighter now raising his fists in the ring.

Now came Billy with his entourage. Billy, head down, hands on Jackie's shoulders ahead of him, looked neither right nor left, acknowledged nothing, but danced on his toes as Jackie pushed ahead through the aisle.

With their arrival, the crowd raised its tumultuous voice even more. Throughout the arena, fists were raised in support and waved in opposition.

T.J. was frightened by the noise and disposition of the crowd. He kept as close to Billy as he possibly could, for he had the eerie feeling that if he became separated from the Champ here, he might never find him again. The mass of people flanking the aisle, some of them standing on their seats, waved and shouted and reached to touch Billy. Swirling smoke from a thousand cigarettes and cigars formed a haze around them all. To T.J. it was as if this surrounding sea might swallow them all up. From this hellish din, single voices reached them:

"Whip this boy's behind, Billy!"

"You the boss!"

"Go back to the horse farm, you bum!"

"Go get him, Flynn!"

"There he is! There he is!"

"Show him who's the champ, Billy!"

"He ain't gonna last two rounds!"

While Billy and his handlers seemed oblivious to all this, T.J. was not. He couldn't tell who the crowd was for, who wasn't gonna last two rounds, and the taunts hurt him. He wished desperately that he could see or hear Josie and Jeffy and the others from the backstretch who were certainly within that horrendous mob somewhere, and would certainly be cheering themselves hoarse.

It seemed like an eternity before they finally reached the ring and climbed the steps to safety, though it was only a couple of minutes.

T.J. stayed on the ring apron, holding onto the ropes, while Billy and the others went through the ropes into the ring. Now Billy, looking across the ring at Bowers, raised his hands to acknowledge the cheers. Shrugging his black robe off into Jackie's hands, he continued to stare across at Bowers.

Bowers was waving and smiling and nodding to his fans as he bounced on his thick legs, rolled his bull neck, and flexed his powerful arms. He was stockier than Billy, sturdier. Obviously he was built more for power than for speed.

Georgie massaged Billy's shoulders as the Champ danced on his toes, arched his back, worked his head from side to side, and shook his dangling hands to loosen up. He lifted his left foot so that Jackie, kneeling in front of him, could scratch the sole of the new shoe with the point of a scissors so that he wouldn't slip. The procedure was repeated with the right foot. Georgie applied Vaseline around Billy's eyes and over his cheekbones, making the skin slick and more difficult to cut.

Hesh held out the left glove, and Billy slid his hand into it; the same with the right. Hesh laced them up.

T.J. could see Billy's cornermen talking and Billy nodding, but couldn't hear their words over the crowd.

Now into the center of the ring walked a small man in a black tuxedo, carrying a sheet of paper in one hand. He waited for the microphone to be lowered to him on a cable, took it in his other hand, glanced at his notes, and said, his voice booming through the arena:

"Ladies and gentlemen!" The crowd quieted a bit. "Ladies and gentlemen!" The crowd quieted more.

Billy had his back to the man, leaning on his forearms over the corner ropes.

"Remember, Billy," Jackie said anxiously, "we don't care about the first three rounds. Stay away, feel him out. He tries to catch guys early. Dope him out, move on him, and we'll catch him later. Okay?"

Billy nodded.

T.J. reached through the ropes to touch Billy's arm. "Champ, you're gonna make him look stupid out there."

"Ladies and gentlemen! In this corner"—the announcer pivoted and held out a hand toward Billy—"weighing one hundred and eighty-three pounds, wearing green trunks with a white stripe, the former light heavyweight champion of the world, Billy—*Flynn!*"

A new and mighty roar went up from the crowd. Billy nodded around and waved his fists briefly.

"And in this corner," the announcer motioned, "weighing one hundred and ninety-two pounds and undefeated in twenty-three fights, Roland—*Bowers!*"

The crowd renewed its commotion of cheers and boos.

Jackie grabbed Billy's wrist and leaned close to him. "He's comin' in light, Billy! He's usually at one ninety-seven or more! He's scared of your *speed*, Billy!"

Billy opened his mouth to receive the mouthpiece, and Jackie slipped it in. Billy worked it around with his tongue.

"The referee is Mike Curtis," the ring announcer went on. "The judges are Mel Berger and Al Heim. Richard Curran is the knockdown timekeeper, and the house physician is Dr. Peter Felcher."

"You got the *reach* on him, Billy!" Hesh said.

The announcer released the mike, and it was drawn up as he left the ring.

The referee came to the center and motioned for the two fighters to join him for instructions.

They came face to face, Bowers looking directly at Billy as if trying to burn a hole in him with his eyes while he chewed his mouthpiece. Billy kept his eyes lowered while Jackie worked the muscles of his neck with his hand.

"Okay, you boys both know the rules," the referee said. "I want a nice clean fight. Protect yourselves at all times. Watch the heads. I'm gonna be looking for butts. You hear me say 'break,' it means just that. Okay, shake hands and come out at the bell."

The two fighters touched gloves and went back to their corners.

"Side to side, Billy," Jackie said, rubbing Billy's back. "Always moving. He's clumsy, he'll tire. Keep him moving and missing, Billy."

The ten-second buzzer sounded, and the cornermen ducked out through the ropes.

Billy held his gloves out to T.J. T.J. put his small hands on them, and he and Billy smiled and nodded to each other in this prearranged gesture of luck.

The house lights dimmed, leaving only those over the ring. The bell sounded for round one.

Bowers bolted across the ring, almost trapping

Billy in his corner. Billy slipped out, circling to his right, his left jab snapping Bowers's head back. Bowers went after him, and Billy kept him off with three quick jabs in a flurry that brought a cheer from his part of the crowd.

Bowers continued to bore in, crouched low, ducking his head, feeling for Billy with light jabs, looking for an opening for the right.

"He ain't nothin' but a boy, Billy!" Georgie yelled. "Teach him! You're the master!"

"He can't touch ya, Champ!" T.J. screeched at the same time. "He's a sucker!"

Billy circled steadily to his right, away from Bowers's dangerous right hand, and peppered the heavier man with left jabs. Then suddenly Billy set his feet and ripped a good short left-right combination to the head. Just as quickly he was back on his toes, dancing out of reach.

Bowers wiped a glove across his nose and moved in. He worked Billy into a corner, then lunged. Billy ducked the right, and Bowers rammed into the ropes awkwardly. Billy pivoted on him and banged two stiff lefts to the side of his head at the bell.

The crew went busily to work in Billy's corner. Jackie took out his mouthpiece as Billy sat down on the stool. Jackie kneaded his thighs and rubbed his belly as he talked.

"You did fine, Billy, just beautiful. He's missing, thinking right hand too much."

Hesh gave him a swig of water and held out the can for him to spit into. Georgie greased his eyebrows.

"Jesus he's strong," Billy said, panting. "Faster than I figured."

"Stay away from him," Jackie said, "just like you been doing. Let him throw all the wild stuff. He's makin' a mistake going after you so early."

"Yeah. He don't hit hard as I thought." Billy was getting his breath now.

"He's trying to wrestle. He's strong inside. Stay away from him."

T.J. took the water bottle from Hesh, and as he turned to put it down, he saw Annie.

None of those with Billy had seen Annie come in during the round. She had rushed down the aisle to take her seat near the ring when the fight was two minutes old. She smiled and waved to T.J., who grinned and waved cheerily back.

"He's tough, Billy," Jackie went on, "but you're doing beautiful. Keep that jab on his nose, and—"

"Champ!" T.J. yelled. "Look, she's here! She's here!"

Billy whipped his head around to look where T.J. was pointing. Annie raised a clenched hand in salute. Billy stared at her.

"Hey, Billy!" Jackie barked. "This ain't broad time! For crissake, snap out of it! *Concentrate!*"

Billy was momentarily stunned. In that moment his last fight appeared before him, that last sad, strange time he had been in the ring. When for five rounds, as she watched him, he had picked apart the challenger to his crown. When he had been at the top of his business, the peak of his talent. That last fight when, after the fifth round, Billy, sitting on his stool in the corner just like now, had looked around at her seat and found her gone, her seat empty. Gone. And when, that time, he had gone out for the sixth round as if in a dream, not caring what happened, not caring if he got hit, going straight at the man he had till then been beating up so handily, walking straight into that right hand and finding himself flat on his back on the canvas and hearing the referee say, ". . . eight, nine, ten and out!" Gone. The title was gone and he didn't care, because she was gone.

All that flashed by in a second. The ten-second buzzer brought him back.

". . . dropping his right," Jackie was saying, "and that's what we're looking for. Okay"—he shoved the mouthpiece between Billy's teeth—"keep moving, don't get cocky, and stay away."

The bell rang, the fighters came out for the second round. It began much like the first, Bowers hurrying across, Billy slipping away and circling, popping him with jabs. Bowers kept coming, crouching, bobbing his thick shoulders and head, pawing with his left, keeping the right cocked. Billy kept him off balance with feints and jabs.

He felt the old grace returning, knew his moves were becoming more fluid as the minutes went by. Bowers lunged. Billy slipped the left at his head, blocked with his elbow the right aimed at his midsection. Bowers could hit; that right numbed his elbow briefly. But Bowers couldn't hit *him*, not where he wanted to. Billy was too quick, too graceful.

Bowers lumbered in, taking the jabs to his head and apparently disdainful of Billy's power. That was a mistake. Billy could hit too, and with much more precision. It would come. He had to be patient and keep moving.

Billy stepped inside a Bowers right and drove a left-right combination to the belly and another to the ribs. Bowers grabbed him in a clinch. The referee separated them at the bell.

"I got him!" Billy rasped after he had spit out his mouthpiece. "He's all mine!" He sat on the stool.

"I saw it," Jackie said, rubbing Billy's arms. "He's bothered by that jab. You're stinging him. He thinks he can ignore it but he can't. You got the reach on him, and it stings."

"You're winning, Champ!" T.J. yelped. "You're beatin' him! You're fightin' great!"

"Now, he's young, Billy," Jackie said, while Billy drank from the bottle and spit out, "so he'll make mistakes. What we do is keep concentrating. We don't get careless."

Billy nodded, then held his head still while Georgie rubbed on the grease.

"Two rounds, Billy, eight to go. So don't get careless. Plenty o' time to do what you can do. Let him bring the fight, just like we planned. Stay away. He's a big boy."

"Strong. I don't want him wrestling me."

"Right. On your toes, in and out, jab, jab, jab. Those inside combos were great. That'll slow him down."

Georgie leaned in. "He's puffy under the left eye already, Billy. Work on that."

Billy nodded as the buzzer sounded. He stood up, Georgie pulled the stool away, and he leaned back against the ropes, spreading his arms across the top strand.

"Let's go, Champ!" T.J. reached up to touch Billy's glove.

This time, at the bell, Billy moved out more quickly, meeting Bowers in the center of the ring and stinging him with two jabs. Then, just as before, he circled, eluding Bowers's attempts to come in under the jab or maneuver him into the ropes.

As Bowers crouched and bobbed low to come in, Billy chopped down on his forehead with a right. Bowers tried to counter with a long, looping left that missed badly.

Bowers continued trying to bull his way in. The red welt grew under his eye, and Billy worked on it, bouncing the quick jab off it as often as he could. Eventually the eye would start to close.

Billy could see that Bowers was growing impatient. He was showing his inexperience. If things went on this way, Billy would win the fight easily on a decision even if he didn't knock Bowers out. He was piling up points with his jab and quick combinations, while Bowers was missing and tiring himself out.

Bowers hurled a looping overhand right. Billy side-stepped it and stepped inside to rip a left to the belly and then a lightning right-left to the head. Bowers's knees buckled, he staggered back a step. He was wobbly, covering up. Billy went at him. Two left jabs between Bowers's gloves found the nose. He came underneath Bowers's elbows with a right to the heart. Then the hook. Billy's left hook caught Bowers clean in front of the ear, and he was down.

The crowd was on its feet, wild at the sight of the knockdown.

Bowers rolled over and got to his knees at the count of six, pushed his gloves against the canvas, and was up at the count of eight.

The referee stepped in front of Bowers to look into his eyes and wipe the gloves off against his shirt. "Go!" He waved the fighters back into action.

"Fifteen seconds!" Jackie yelled.

Billy came out of the neutral corner looking to set Bowers up for one more shot. But Bowers, crouched, holding his gloves together in front of his face, bulled Billy back against the ropes. He leaned his head against Billy's chest and worked both hands to the body as the bell sounded.

"How you feel?" Jackie asked as he kneaded Billy's biceps.

"Good—feel good—okay."

"Get your breath now, take it easy."

"Strong—arms like iron—See me knock him down? —He went down."

"Yeah, yeah, and he got back up. He's tough. Gotta be patient. You'll have another chance. Wait him out. Still wait him out."

"Strong, like Richie Soll. Reminds me of Richie Soll."

"Forget Soll, for crissake! This is Bowers! Concentrate, Billy, don't lose your concentration. How's your gut?"

"Good—He ain't hurtin' me none."

"Don't let him work downstairs like that. He'll take too much outta ya."

"Feel great."

The ten-second buzzer sounded.

"Hey, Champ!" T.J. called through the ropes. "He was out on his feet! You got him, Champ!"

"Stay off him till you got a opening, Billy. Okay, let's go!"

Billy glanced down to Annie, then stood up, heard the bell, and moved quickly out.

Billy tried a straight right lead, but Bowers had recovered enough to duck under it. He wasn't coming in now, he was more cautious. But neither was he backing off and covering up. Bowers pawed out with his left hand, Billy swiping it away with his glove. Apparently Bowers was stalling, wanting to recover fully before going back on the attack.

After a minute had gone, Bowers again waded in. He threw a wild right and a wild left, both missing Billy's head but both thudding into his shoulders, backing him up. Bowers bulled him into the ropes. Billy tried to slide away to his right, but Bowers stayed on him, digging his fists into the body. Then, as Billy ducked a left, Bowers caught him with a grazing but powerful right that opened a cut over Billy's left eye.

Billy danced off the ropes and began to circle, swiping at the cut with his glove and staying away from Bowers. The referee signaled for time and stepped between the fighters. He took Billy's head in his hands and looked at the cut.

"Okay, it's okay," the ref said, motioning them together again.

The cut unnerved Billy. He was seldom cut. The worst way to lose a fight was from a cut, when they might stop it even though you felt fine.

The cut stimulated Bowers. Now he had a target. If Billy had built up a commanding lead in the early rounds, and Bowers couldn't catch him to knock him out, he could at least work on that cut. He charged at Billy, sending overhand lefts and rights at him, homing in on that widening slice over Billy's eye.

Blood trickled down both sides of the eye. Billy didn't know how bad the cut was. The referee was keeping watch on it as he moved around the ring. Billy was scared. Rather than continue to rely on his clever movement and quicker jabs, he moved less and loaded up with heavier punches, looking for a knockout.

The tempo of the fight changed, and at the end of the round they were toe to toe, slugging it out. The roaring of the crowd almost drowned out the bell.

Billy dropped onto his stool, his chest heaving. Georgie worked furiously on his eyes with anticoagulant and Q-Tips.

"You gotta stay away from him, Billy!" Jackie said urgently. "Listen now! You stay the hell away!"

"How bad?—how bad?—"

"Keep him away from it, you'll be all right."

T.J. felt nauseous, looking at the gash over Billy's eye. He swallowed several times. But he couldn't take his eyes off it. Even when Georgie stemmed the bleeding, the cut looked raw and ugly. T.J. couldn't speak to him this time between rounds.

The referee came over and leaned in for a look at the eye. He nodded and walked away. Georgie had done his work well.

"He'll be goin' for that," Jackie said, "and you know it. You're not listening to me! Stop looking around for that broad! Concentrate! Don't get cute on me, now. You don't have the power to handle this guy inside. You can't slug with him, he's strong, Billy!"

"Had him—I had him—"

"This fight is yours if you listen to me. Wait your spot. Don't have to knock him out. Stick and move, stick and move, keep him away from that eye!"

As round five began, Billy felt uncertain for the first time. He hadn't figured on getting cut. And Bowers could take a punch, that was certain, and could come back. Billy was not so light on his feet, and for an instant he wondered about his age.

Bowers came out as before, low, hulking, scowling at Billy. Bowers ignored a couple of jabs and lunged inside, driving a left and right into Billy's ribs. Then he stepped back and swung that overhand right, catching Billy's eye, reopening the cut and sending a crimson shower over the mat.

Billy instantly countered with two wild punches of his own, blindly trying to fight Bowers off.

"Stay the hell away!" Jackie screamed. "*Box* him, Billy!"

"Champ!" T.J. screamed in a high, weak voice. "Champ! Champ!"

Hesh had to restrain him at the ropes.

The crowd was perpetually on its feet now, smelling a climax, most of them howling with pleasure at the action. A few of them, though—like Annie—were unable to watch the flow of blood, and turned away.

Billy didn't hear anything from the corner. He was caught up in a panic. Blood gushed over his eye, nearly blinding him. Again and again he launched roundhouse punches hoping to catch Bowers with a lucky one that would end it. Bowers plowed in, aiming for the eye.

The ref called for time and stepped between them. This time he took Billy's arm and led him to ringside and called for the boxing commission doctor.

"I'm okay—" Billy gasped, "okay—I'm okay—"

Blood ran down Billy's face and dripped off his chin. The doctor, looking strangely out of place with his neat gray hair and pin stripe suit, held Billy's face in his hands to study the eye. He worked his fingers around the cut to gauge its extent.

The doctor nodded to the referee, and the ref signaled the fighters to go ahead.

By trying to slug it out with him, Billy was playing right into Bowers's hands. Bowers bobbed and weaved and moved in behind a succession of murderous punches to Billy's midsection. Then, as Billy covered up with his elbows, Bowers went for the opening with his booming right uppercut.

Billy was down. He didn't feel hurt. He heard the count. He was surprised and a little numb, but he wasn't hurt. He got to his feet at the count of six and shook his head disgustedly.

Bowers was on him right away. Billy felt okay, but his legs were strangely rubbery. He couldn't dance away. He tried to fend Bowers off with short rights, but Bowers ignored them and kept coming. Billy wanted desperately to find an opening for the left hook, but the blood blurred his vision. While he was looking, Bowers hooked a left of his own, catching Billy flush on the jaw and dropping him for the second time, just as the bell sounded.

Under the rules, he wouldn't be saved by the bell. The count continued as Billy, more hurt this time, struggled to get to his feet. Blood now filled his nose too, making it difficult to breathe.

He made it up at eight, and Georgie and Jackie rushed out to help him back to his corner.

"I wanna stop it now, Champ," Jackie said as Georgie worked frantically on the cut. "I wanna stop it."

"No—no—" Blood trickled out of his mouth. "This

round I got him—" The words came out hoarsely between gasps.

Tears rolled down T.J.'s face as he watched stricken from outside the ropes. "Champ . . . Champ . . ."

"I'm sayin' please, Billy," Jackie persisted, "I'm sayin' please here, lemme stop it. I don't want you scrambled, Billy, it ain't worth it."

"No—no—I'm okay—got him this round—" He tried to shake his head, but Georgie held it still, trying to work on the cut.

The doctor came into the ring and bent down in front of Billy with the referee. Georgie had done his job expertly; the blood was stopped. The skin showed a cruel gap, but it wasn't bleeding and the eye was still partly open.

"It doesn't look good," the doctor said to the referee, "but he can see. I'll let him go for a while." He stepped away.

The referee remained, looking into Billy's eyes. "Billy, what day is it, Billy?"

"I'm okay—Wednesday—no, Thursday—It's Thursday." Billy tried to open his eyes wider but was blinded by the ring lights.

"Where are we, Billy?"

"Forum—Forum—Miami."

"You wanna go more?"

"Yeah—I'm okay—Lemme fight—Don't stop it—"

T.J. leaned through the ropes, shivering with quiet sobs. "Please, Champ, please, don't fight no more, please, Champ—"

"Okay," the referee said to Jackie, "I seen worse, so I'll let him go. He goes down again, it's over."

Billy forced himself up off the stool at the sound of the buzzer.

"I won't let him butcher you, Champ," Jackie said as he climbed out through the ropes. "I swear I won't let him butcher you!"

The bell rang for the sixth round. Billy plodded out. This was *the* round, the sixth. Last time it was the sixth that finished him. The sixth. He had given up in the sixth, last time. But not this time. He would never give up in this round. Last time she was gone. This time she was still here. She was out there in the crowd, he saw her. She was crying, but broads always cry. She was there. And T.J. was there. Billy could hear him.

"Champ . . . Champ . . ."

He collided with Bowers and they both swung wildly, their gloves thudding off each other's heads and chins and shoulders and arms. Billy was throwing punches he had never thrown before, like a drunken street-fighter. He was groggy and tired, his legs were gone, he was old. . . .

But suddenly Jackie's words were with him again, right in his head: *Box him, Billy, jab him, when he dips that right shoulder for the uppercut, then you throw the left hook . . . You got the best left hook God created, Billy . . .*

"Champ . . . Champ . . ."

Billy backed off, somehow got up on his toes to move, to circle. He bounced two left jabs off Bowers's cheekbone. Bowers was more clumsy than ever coming in. He was tired. He dipped the right shoulder. Billy put everything he had left into the left hook.

He didn't see what happened. Bowers staggered backwards and fell against the ropes and slid down, one hand futilely grasping for the lower strand. He lay there, one arm over the ropes, eyes closed, one leg flat, the other cocked up.

Billy didn't see that. He sagged back against the ropes himself, still standing but powerless. When he heard the referee count ". . . seven, eight, nine . . ." he could open but one eye. The cut eye was swollen shut. Through his one good eye Billy saw that Bowers

217

was on his side, reaching for the middle rope to pull himself up, when the referee said, "ten!"

Billy saw the referee spread his arms over Bowers, and he saw the referee then come over to him. The ref took Billy's right hand and raised it high. Blood from Billy's own face ran down that arm. Billy looked at Bowers, but the view was swimming in front of him. The whole arena was tilting crazily. He felt as if he were floating.

T.J. reached him first, hugging him around the waist. Jackie, Georgie, and Hesh surrounded him and hugged him and raised his fists for him.

Billy pushed away from them and floated over to Bowers's corner. Bowers was sitting on his stool, sagging with defeat. "Goofight," Billy mumbled through his bloody mouthpiece as he rubbed his glove on the top of Bowers's downcast head. "Goofight."

Everything was spinning. He let them lead him away.

"No interviews!" Jackie barked at the reporters as he pushed ahead to clear the way out of the ring and down the steps. "No interviews right now! Later!"

"Are ya okay, Champ?" T.J. cried. "Jackie, is the Champ okay?"

Jackie brushed by him. Billy was in lockstep behind Jackie, his still-gloved hands on Jackie's shoulders. "Let us through there!" Jackie shouted. "Make way, we're comin' through! Come on, move it!"

Two policemen formed a wedge in front of Jackie and cleared a path up the aisle.

Jackie's face was rigid. He hadn't even taken the time to cut Billy's gloves off. He had to get him inside to the table.

"Is he okay, Jackie?" T.J. called desperately from behind, holding the fine black robe tightly against his chest. "Is the Champ okay?"

Blood still dripped from Billy's nose and chin. His

eyes were closed. He stumbled blindly behind Jackie.

"Billy!" It was Annie's voice from somewhere. "Billy!" He tried to open his eyes. He nodded. He was floating.

In the dressing room, they lay Billy down on the rubbing table. Georgie held smelling salts under his nose. Billy coughed and opened his one good eye, He pushed himself into a sitting position.

"Easy, Billy," Jackie said.

"I'm okay." He seemed much revived. He wasn't floating any more. A little dizzy, maybe, but okay. "I got a list—of people I made bets with—about—" He coughed again, a deep, hoarse cough that made tiny bubbles in the blood oozing around his teeth. "Fifteen thousand bucks worth. It's in my pocket—over there, Jackie."

"Later, Billy. Let's get to the shower and get the hell out of here to the hospital and have 'em check that eye."

"No—no—important." Billy pushed himself off the table and stood wavering beside it. "Tonight—gotta collect tonight."

He stumbled, and Georgie grabbed him. "Billy, you all right? Jackie, his eyes don't look right."

"No, they don't."

Charlie Goodman barged into the room, chewing on a new cigar and beaming merrily. "Helluva fight, Billy! Super show! We gotta talk, Billy. Tomorrow. That kid from New York I was telling you about. I think he'll sign now." He tapped Billy's arm playfully with a fist. "God bless you, Billy. Helluva fight. We're on our way!"

"Get the hell outta here, Charlie!" Jackie snapped, pushing him away. "Billy ain't good."

"T.J.?" Billy looked around, trying to focus.

"Yeah, Champ, I'm right here, Champ!"

"You got any aspirin?"

"What, Champ? I can hardly hear you."

"Aspirin. Gimme couple . . ." His eyes closed slowly and he started to fall.

Jackie and Hesh grabbed him under the arms and held him up, moving him toward the table.

"Doctor!" Jackie yelled. "Somebody get the doctor!"

"Please, Champ!" T.J. tried to help hold him up. "It's gonna be all right, Champ! Please, Champ, please . . ."

There was a crowd at the door.

"Doctor!" Jackie screamed. "Where the hell's a goddam doctor!"

They hauled Billy's limp form up onto the rubbing table and lay him down. His eyelids fluttered.

"Legs . . ." he said weakly, "just gave out . . . coupla aspirin . . ."

"Champ, please, Champ!" T.J. tried to smooth Billy's matted hair. "They called a doctor, Champ! It's gonna be okay, Champ!"

"Don't need no . . . doctor . . . just lay down . . . dizzy . . ."

"Get that crowd the hell outta here!" Jackie yelled. "This ain't no freak show! Get 'em out! Where's the damn doctor?"

Annie was trying to push through the mob outside the room. "Let me through! Get out of my way!"

"You can't go in there, lady," the cop said.

"Don't tell me I can't go in there!" She was nearly hysterical, her hands clenched at her chest. "He's my . . . my . . . *husband!*"

The cop stepped aside, letting her pass, then resumed his stance to block the rest of the pushing crowd. He started to shut the door behind him, when the doctor appeared, holding up his black bag to show the cop who he was. The cop let him wedge through the door, then closed it after him. Annie started for the table where the Champ lay, then edged off to the side, discreetly staying out of the way, her hands clenched white in front of her, while the doctor went to the table.

The overhead lights glistening off his sweating bald head, the doctor stooped and nervously opened his bag on the floor beside Billy. His hands shook and he fumbled his tools, feeling around the bag for the stethoscope and muttering under his breath.

Billy lay still, his right hand holding T.J.'s right. His voice was even lower than before. "T.J., you there?"

"Right here, Champ! It's gonna be—"

"Hey, that was . . . beautiful, wasn't it? Huh, T.J.? You see . . . what I did out there . . . T.J.?"

"Yeah, Champ!" He tried to hold back the tears, but they flooded down anyway. "I never saw nothin' like that, Champ! Nobody ever saw a fighter like you!"

"Whaddaya think they'll . . . put in the papers?"

"They'll say . . . they'll say you were the best ever, Champ! They'll say you could box and punch and, and, and dance and move! They'll say you came back for real! For *real*! They'll say—"

T.J. felt the strength ebbing in Billy's hand. "No, Champ! Everything's gonna be all right! Hang on, Champ!" He gripped harder with his own hand. "Don't let go, Champ!"

"Everything's . . . gonna . . ." His voice dropped off. He started to raise his hand, and T.J. released it. Billy raised his hand in a fist until it was under T.J.'s chin. "T.J. . . . you gotta . . . always keep . . . your chin . . . up and . . . be . . . be . . . strong. . . ."

With each word Billy pushed T.J.'s chin higher, until T.J.'s head was arched back. "Okay, Champ," he said with difficulty. "Oh jeez, somebody help . . ."

Then Billy's hand dropped. His arm hung limp down from the table. "Champ! Champ!"

The doctor quickly put his stethoscope to Billy's chest and at the same time with his thumb pushed up one of Billy's eyelids. "Sorry," the doctor said, shaking his head, "this man's dead."

T.J. hurled himself over Billy's still form, trying desperately to crawl up onto the table. "No! No! God, please! The Champ ain't dead! He can't be! Champ! Please, Champ!"

Jackie dragged him off, wrapped his arms tightly around him and pulled him back from the table.

T.J. struggled hysterically. "Champ! Champ! Everything's gonna be okay, Champ! You don't haveta talk! I want you with me, Champ! You ain't dead! The Champ ain't dead!"

He fought blindly against Jackie's hold, his screams muddled with sobs.

"He's gone, kid," Jackie said, his own face covered with tears.

"He ain't! I want him! Champ!"

Georgie's arms joined Jackie's around T.J. "T.J., please, boy, please. Ain't nothin' nobody can—" His own voice was choked off by sobs.

"T.J." It was Annie. "T.J." She held her arms open to him.

Suddenly T.J. stopped fighting. He stood looking at her. Jackie let him go. He took a step toward her. Then he lunged for her, falling into her arms.

"Please hold me, Annie," he wept.

"Yes, T.J." She pressed him to her as tightly as she could, forgetting for the moment her own despair.

"Hold me just like the Champ, Annie. Hold me like the Champ."

"Always, T.J. I'll hold you. Just like the Champ."